MY CITY

Jason T. Seals

Dedicate

To

L.C. SEALS

&

Susie Seals

CONTENTS

CHAPTER 1

"Quincy, will you please slow down?!"

"Quinn, if I slow down, we'll miss the graduation."

"You are driving like a bat out of hell. If you keep driving like this, we won't be alive to go to the graduation. We will end up in the morgue," Quinn said as she laughed.

"Whatever, Quinn! Look, we're pulling up on the campus now."

"Quincy, the auditorium is on the other side of the campus."

"Well, it looks like we have to run to make it on time."

"WHAT DO YOU MEAN, RUN?! Quincy, I am wearing a dress and some damn heels."

"Well, take them off when you run. Look, Quinn, the ceremony starts in fifteen minutes. If you want to make it in time, we have to run to the auditorium!"

So Quincy and Quinn started running, trying to make it before the ceremony started. They had to run through the quad in order to make it to the other side of the campus.

They got there just in time. As soon they walked into the auditorium, they were calling Quincy's name to come up and get his diploma.

Quincy was so excited to be getting his college degree. He was the first one in his family to go to college.

After Quinn's name was called, Quincy and Quinn were about to slip out and meet up with their parents when Professor Jeff Williams took the mic and began making a special announcement.

"I know that this is not protocol, yet I would be remiss if I did not recognize this young man," the professor said. "We have an award for him. When he first arrived here at Harvard University, he had such a hard time getting started. Most of his classmates gave him a hard time as well. Yet this young man kept pushing and working, striving, making sure he kept up with his classwork, getting nothing but straight A's on all the exams. He never gave up.

"Yet what really made this young man stand out was the fact that the same people that gave him a hard time ended up asking him for help with their classwork. He showed great humility and kindness towards the same people who were very cruel and downright nasty to him. Those same people would end up becoming his friends.

"This young man's name is Quincy Black."

Just as Quincy was trying to sneak out of the auditorium, Professor Williams called Quincy's name. Everybody was cheering and clapping for him. Quincy was kind of surprised that his professor would convince the rest of the staff to give him an award like this.

After Quincy went up on stage to receive his award, the entire school stood up and gave him a standing ovation. Everyone started chanting, "Speech! Speech! Speech!"

Quincy started his speech by saying, "When I received my acceptance letter from Harvard Law School, I was told that Harvard would not expect me. I was told that Massachusetts was not a place for a young black man. When I arrived here at Harvard, I was met with so much hatred and cruelty. It made me question why I had come here to study law. I could have gone to Oxford or to any black college, where I would've been accepted. Yet Harvard has the best law program in the country. So I knew that I was in the right place.

"One day I was having a very bad day. Nothing was going right. Everything you could think of was going wrong. I just wasn't going to take it anymore. I had put in a transfer to another college.

"Professor Williams asked me to stay after class one day. He pulled me to the side and said, 'So I hear that you are transferring to another school.' I replied that I was. He asked me why, and I told him that no matter how hard I tried or how good my grades were, it felt like I was being bullied and targeted for no reason at all.

"Professor Williams looked at me and started laughing. He said, 'Quincy, the reason why you are being picked on and targeted is because they see potential and greatness in you. That's why they are trying to stop you. They want you to quit; most of them are jealous of you. Even some of the professors are jealous of you.'

"He also said, 'Quincy, don't quit. You keep pushing and making good grades. If those same students and teachers keep giving you a hard time, don't return the favor. You do the opposite. God will turn your enemies into your footstools.'

"So I took my professor's advice. I stayed here at Harvard, while my fellow students—the ones that were giving me a hard time—either transferred or got kicked out. Even some of the professors left.

"I started making friends. Even some of those that gave me a hard time before started asking me for help with their work. After a period of time, they became my good friends.

"Staying here at Harvard was one of the best decisions that I ever made. If I had left, I wouldn't have met my beautiful fiancée, Quinn!"

Everyone started to laugh.

Quincy finished his speech by saying, "Before I take my seat, I just want to thank Harvard and Professor Williams for this honor. Thank you from the bottom of my heart." As Quincy started to leave the stage, everyone stood up and cheered and clapped for him.

Right after the announcement, the dean said, "I give you the class of nineteen sixty-five!"

As everybody was celebrating, Quincy was looking for Quinn. He finally caught up with her. To his surprise, his mother was standing right next to Quinn with Quinn's parents. Quincy was so shocked, he dropped his hat and started hugging her.

"Mama, how did you get here?"

"Well, Quincy, your beautiful fiancée arranged for me to be here with you."

"Quinn, how did you plan this behind my back?"

"Well, Quincy, I asked my mother and father to loan me the money for a plane ticket for your mother to come see you receive your degree. Mom and Dad told me that I didn't have to ask to borrow anything. They said that they would be happy to pay for your mom to come to your graduation."

"I don't know what to say, Quinn!" Quincy said as tears ran down his face. Mary, Quincy's mother, wiped away his tears.

Professor Williams went over to give Quincy and Quinn a hug. "I am really proud of the both of you," he said. "Quinn, I told you he was going to be alright."

"Wait a minute, how long have you two been talking about me?" Quincy asked.

"Sweetie, that's between Professor Williams and me," Quinn

said as she gave Quincy a kiss.

"Hey, Professor, you have to come to dinner with us."

"Quincy, I don't know about that. I wouldn't want to impose on any family time."

"Professor Williams, you *are* family."

"OK Quinn, OK Quincy! I will come. You know I never could say no to you two."

As everyone was at the restaurant, having a good time, Professor Williams asked Quincy a question. "So, Quincy, have you thought about my offer?"

"What offer?" Quinn asked.

"Well, Quinn, Mama, Professor Williams has made me a job offer at his law firm, here in Boston."

"What is there to think about, Quincy?!" Mama Mary asked.

"Mama, I actually thought about coming back to Kansas City, so I can be close to you."

"Don't worry about me. You are about to start a family. You don't even know if you can get a job in Kansas City or not. You better not turn down a guaranteed job."

"Mama!"

"Don't you 'Mama' me, Quincy. Things are changing, but they are not changing overnight. Things are not getting any better in Kansas City. If a black man has a chance to get a really good job for what he went to school for, he better take it."

"Well, Mama, how about this? I have a couple of interviews back in Kansas City." Turning to the professor, he said, "I will let you know in a couple of days, Professor Williams."

"OK, Quincy, that seems fair."

"Quincy, please stay here in Massachusetts. Please take Professor Williams's offer."

"Mama, I am going to weigh out all of my options first."

"Quincy, do you actually think that they are going to let a black man work as a lawyer in Kansas City? No law firm in Kansas City is going to hire you, sweetie. I don't want you and Quinn to struggle like your father and I did."

"Mama, if I have an opportunity to practice law in my home-town, I am going to take it. I want to make a difference in the community, my community."

"I understand how you feel, Quincy, I really do. But Quincy, no man or woman should have to struggle to help his community. I know you have dream of becoming a big-time lawyer in your own hometown, but you need to wake up."

CHAPTER 2

W hile Quincy and Quinn were packing, getting ready to head back to Kansas City, Missouri, Quincy had a worried look on his face.

"Quincy, what's wrong, sweetheart?"

"Nothing, Quinn! I'm alright."

"We have been together long enough for me to know when you are not telling me the truth."

"Quinn, really! OK! OK! I'm kind of worried about the interview back in Kansas City. I wonder what will happen if they don't hire me."

"Even if you don't get a job, you out of all people should know that God is not going to leave us hanging. He didn't bring us this far to leave us. We will be just fine, I know we will. So let's get ready to go and head home," Quinn said, giving him a kiss.

***

Quincy and Quinn had just arrived back in Kansas City, Missouri. Quinn had only been here a couple times with Quincy to visit his mother. Now this time she was moving here with him.

Quincy and Quinn were in the cab, heading to his mother's house from the airport. They were driving through Quincy's old neighborhood. While he was riding home, he looked out the window, remembering all of the things that he did as a kid and as a teenager, the good and the bad. As he was reminiscing, tears started rolling down his face. Most of Quincy's friends were either locked up or had died. It brought tears to Quincy's eyes as he thought about them.

The cab pulled up to his mother's house. Quincy got all of their bags and luggage out of the cab. As Quincy and Quinn walk into his mother's house, everyone shouted at once, "SURPRISE!" Quincy's mother had put together a little surprise welcome-home party for him.

Quincy and Quinn were shocked and surprised. Quincy recognized some of his old friends, cousins, and family members he hadn't seen in a long time. Even the pastor of the church Quincy had attended while he was growing up was there.

Quincy went towards his mother and gave her a big kiss and a hug. After all of the excitement had worn down, Quincy and Quinn were talking, laughing, and having a good time. Quincy introduced Quinn to everybody.

Pastor Banks pulled Quincy to the side so they could talk.

"Thanks for looking after my mother while I was away at school," Quincy said.

"Quincy, you don't have to thank me for that. Your mother is a big part of the church and this community. I am very proud of you, Quincy. The whole community is very proud of you. It's very rare for a black man to graduate from college, but to graduate from Harvard Law School, that is a blessing."

"Thanks, Pastor Banks, I really appreciate that."

"So, Quincy, what are your plans now that you are back in Kansas City?"

"Well, I have a job interview at a law firm downtown."

"Quincy, that is so wonderful! Which law firm are you interviewing with?"

"Johnson and Johnson, one of the most prestigious law firms in Kansas City."

"Quincy, I totally understand why you came back to Kansas City. You getting an interview at all at a dominantly white law firm is very, very impressive. Still, be careful. I don't want you to be disappointed. I've seen a lot of brothers come back from college. Out of all of them, only five, or one percent, actually get into the field that they went to school for."

"Pastor, what happened to them? Did they at least try to find a job in their field?"

"They did try, and all of them were well qualified. They just weren't the right color. As smart as you are, Quincy, I just don't want to see you go through that. I heard about the offer back in Boston. I do realize that Boston is even worse when it comes to hiring blacks, but if you got an offer that leads to a guaranteed job, son, in these days, take it."

"Pastor Banks, if there is just a slight chance that I can practice law here in Kansas City and be close to my mother as well, I *have* to take it. If I don't get the job here at the law firm, then I will consider taking the job back in Boston. I really don't want to leave my mother here in Kansas City by herself."

"Well, Quincy, just wait and see what happens tomorrow at the interview. Then pray and ask the Lord to lead you."

"OK, Pastor Banks."

As Quincy and Pastor Banks finished talking, everybody started to leave the party.

***

It had been a long night for Quincy and Quinn. Quincy, Quinn, and Mary were all tired. Quincy had to get ready for his interview tomorrow, so he took a shower, got his clothes together, and went to bed.

CHAPTER 3

I t was around six a.m., and Quincy was just getting up.

Quinn was really tired. Normally, she would be up before Quincy. Mary was already up, cooking Quincy some breakfast.

"Mama, you didn't have to get up and cook breakfast for me. I was going to grab a donut and some coffee."

"Quincy, don't be silly, you can't go to an interview on an empty stomach. I thought your future wife would have been up cooking you something to eat."

"Mama, leave Quinn alone, she was really tired last night. She is usually up before me."

"I was just joking, Quincy. I figured she was tired."

"Well, wish me luck."

"Quincy, there is no such thing is luck."

"OK, Mama, just pray for me."

"I always do, Quincy."

***

Quincy arrived at the offices of Johnson & Johnson and checked in with the receptionist. As he walked up to the desk, he was told, "Sir, are you in the right place? The welfare office is the next building over."

"Excuse me, I am here for an interview. My appointment is at eight thirty."

"Well, sir, I do apologize, but we don't hire janitors. This a law firm; we only hire lawyers."

"Yes, ma'am, I know. I am a lawyer," he said as he handed her his business card. As she cleared her throat, she asked, "Your name is Quincy Black?" She could not believe it as she read Quincy's card.

"Mr. Black, wait here for one minute."

The receptionist went and got one of the senior lawyers. The senior lawyer came out and asked Quincy, "How can I help you, son?"

"Well, I have an interview at eight thirty. My name is Quincy Black."

"YOU'RE QUINCY BLACK??" the lawyer asked. "So surprising."

"Yes sir."

"Son, follow me." He took Quincy to a conference room. "Can you wait here for a couple of minutes?"

Quincy waited in the conference room for almost two and a half hours. Finally, three associate lawyers went into the conference room with Quincy.

"We are so sorry to have left you waiting so long."

"Not a problem," Quincy said. Quincy was calm and relaxed.

"Mr. Black, your resume is very impressive. So we did some checking, to make sure you are Quincy Black. We called your professor that you studied under. He verified everything that was in your resume. But unfortunately, we already filled the position."

Quincy looked at all three of the associate lawyers and said, "Well, before I go, can you be upfront with me and tell me the real reason why you don't want to hire me?"

"You want the truth? OK, here it is. Out of twenty years that I have been practicing law, there has never been a nigger this damn smart. It's impossible. You had to cheat or you got your professor to lie for you. NEVERTHELESS, NO NIGGER IS GOING TO WORK AT THIS FIRM AS LONG AS I'M ALIVE. NOW GET YOUR BLACK ASS OUT OF MY OFFICE BEFORE I HAVE YOU THROWN OUT," the head lawyer yelled.

Quincy got up, thanked the associate lawyers for their time, and walked out. Quincy was kind of shocked, but yet he wasn't.

On the bus on the way back to his home, he really thought things would be different. He just knew that things were changing for the better. Yet things were not changing fast enough. Quincy realized that he had always wanted to work as a lawyer in his hometown, yet the only way that he was going to be able to be a lawyer and make a decent living was if he accepted the offer from Professor Williams.

Quincy was very disappointed and heartbroken. When he got home, Quinn and Mary wanted to know how his interview went.

"Hey Quincy. So, how did the interview go?" Quinn asked.

Quincy didn't say a word, he just went to the back of the house.

Quinn and Mary knew that something wasn't right.

Quinn went back to check on Quincy. "Baby, are you OK?"

"Well, Quinn, you, Mama, and Pastor Banks were right. They thought that I was a white man from Harvard. When they found out that I was black, they almost had me thrown out of the office. I thought things were changing. I sure was wrong about that. I am so sorry, Quinn, we should've just stayed in Massachusetts."

"Quincy, stop it and quit talking like that. If you want to stay here in Kansas City, then that's what we will do.

"Honey, we will be OK. God got us. We will make it work, trust me." Quinn kissed Quincy before she left the room.

Mary was kind of eavesdropping. As Quinn left the room, Mary went in right after her. "Hey kiddo, I heard what happened!"

Quincy started laughing. "Yeah, I'm quite sure you did."

"Quincy, I want to give you something." She handed him a white envelope full of money.

"Mama, there has to be a least twenty grand or more in here."

"It's thirty grand, Quincy. I have been saving for a while."

"Mama, I can't take this, this is your money."

"This was supposed to be your graduation present. I was going to give it to you back in Massachusetts, but I forgot to. With the ceremony and dinner and excitement, it slipped my mind. I know why I forgot now! I guess it was God's plan for me to give this to you now."

"Mama!"

"Quincy, this is how you become a lawyer in your hometown. You start your own law firm. I will help you as much as I can. I'm quite sure Quinn will too."

"OK, Mama, I will!"

So Quincy took the money that Mary had saved for him. He started his own firm with a little help from Quinn, his mother, and Professor Williams.

CHAPTER 4

I t had been almost two years since Quincy was turned down by Johnson & Johnson Law Firm. He started his own firm in Kansas City, but he also accepted the job offer from Professor Williams as well.

The job with Professor Williams kept Quincy out of town for two or three days a week. The professor put Quincy on a retainer. He got at least twenty thousand dollars a month, which was very generous, and it was a lot of money for a black man to be making in the mid-sixties. It allowed Quincy to stay in Kansas City.

Even though he had his own law firm, Quincy was not getting that much clientele, so the work that he was getting from the professor kept him in business.

After two years, Quincy was thinking about moving his law firm to Boston. Quinn had gotten a job as a clerk for a judge in Kansas City. She would also help out Quincy at his law firm as much as she could.

Quincy, Quinn, and his mother were living pretty comfortably. Yet Quincy wanted to do more for his community. Some of the people in the community that came to him could barely afford a lawyer. Quincy would set them on payment plans or quote them a very cheap fair deal. Yet, even though he was helping his community, Quincy still had to make a living.

While Quincy was wrapping up another case, just as he was leaving the court house, he was approached by a man named James Cantone.

"Hey, is your name Quincy Black?"

"Yes. Yes it is. How can I help you, sir?"

"Well, I have a little tax problem that you can help with. You were recommended by someone who knows you in Boston. I would really appreciate it if you could take a look at this for me, Mr. Black."

"Sure thing, Mr. Cantone."

Quincy went over James's tax problem. The prosecutor was trying to prove that James had not paid his taxes in the past seven years, even though James had proof he had paid his taxes. The lawyer was trying to prove that the tax papers that James had provided were not real and that they had been forged. It took Quincy just two weeks to look over all of the documents.

Quincy called a meeting with his client, James, the prosecutor, and the judge.

"OK, Mr. Black, you called for this meeting?"

"Of course, Your Honor. I would like to put in a motion for all charges to be dropped against my client."

"On what grounds, Mr. Black?"

"On the grounds of how the prosecutor has been dragging this case for the past two years, wasting the taxpayers' money. Also the fact that there is no proof that these documents have been forged. I took the time to make sure that all of these documents are legitimate tax papers, proving that these paid taxes are real. We could take this to trial, given all of the evidence and proof, but I doubt either one of you would want the embarrassment."

"Well, Mr. Black, you bring up a valid point. The only question that I have for my DA is why wasn't this looked over two years ago? Two years is a long time of wasting the taxpayers' money.

If the DA does not have any new evidence, I am dismissing this case."

"Mr. Cantone, all of the charges have been dropped," Quincy told Mr. Cantone.

"Mr. Black, that was very, very impressive. Thank you for taking this case." James handed Quincy a check for one hundred fifty thousand dollars. Quincy looked at the check and thought it was a mistake.

"Mr. Cantone, did you make a mistake?"

"What do you mean, Mr. Black? Was that not enough?"

"Well, Mr. Cantone, you're going to pay me one hundred fifty thousand dollars for just a small tax case?"

"Mr. Black—"

"Please, Mr. Cantone, call me Quincy."

"Quincy, no one that I took this case to would have gotten it dismissed this fast. You made the DA look like a dumbass. You deserve every penny of that check."

"Well, thank you, Mr. Cantone."

"Quincy, please call me James. I might be calling on you for some more cases. Will that be OK, Quincy?

"Sure, when you need me, just let me know, James."

Quincy could not believe it. He had just been paid one hundred fifty thousand dollars for just a small tax case. Quincy thought to himself that this was too good to be true, yet he just went along with the flow.

He went home and told Quinn and Mary what happened. Quincy told both his mother and Quinn to get dressed so he could take them out to dinner.

Mary was kind of suspicious about how much money Quincy was paid for the case. Mary really didn't want to go anywhere, nor did she want Quincy to spend any of that money. Yet she knew that Quincy would not listen to her. So she just kept quiet, and waited for the right time to talk to Quincy.

Quincy took Quinn and Mary to the Herford House downtown. While they were having dinner, all three were having a good time. Quincy's mother, Mary, was not comfortable at all, however. She was enjoying the food, yet she was still uneasy about it.

"Quincy, you should not have taken that money. It just doesn't make any sense for that man to pay you that much money for such a petty case like that."

"Mama, can we just enjoy ourselves for once?"

"Mary, there is no danger, it was just a tax case. If a client wants to be generous and pay Quincy that much for a case like this, what's wrong with that?" Quinn pointed out.

"You two are so stupid and naïve."

"MAMA, REALLY!" Quincy said.

Quincy whispered to the waitress to bring Mary a glass of bourbon. The waitress brought the drink and set it down right between Quincy and his mother. While Mary was drinking her water, Quincy switched her drink. When Mary started drinking, she started eating a lot as well.

"Quincy, did you just give your mother a glass of bourbon?" Quinn asked.

"Yep, I sure did, and I'm about to order her another glass."

Quincy ordered Mary about three glasses of bourbon. By the time Quinn, Quincy, and Mary got home, Mary was so drunk that she was out like a light. Quincy and Quinn put Mary to bed.

Quincy asked Quinn, "Hey, Quinn, do you want to go to Boston?"

"When, tonight? For real? What about Mama?"

"She's knocked out. I can get one of my cousins to come over and watch her while we are gone. Quinn, if you want to go, don't pack anything, let's just go to the airport and go. If we need some clothes, we can buy some more in Boston."

"Okay, Quincy, let's go."

And so Quincy and Quinn flew to Boston for the weekend.

CHAPTER 5

Quinn and Quincy had flown to Boston on Friday night just to get out of town for the weekend. The only time that Quincy had been out town was for business. This time Quincy was going to Boston with Quinn to enjoy himself.

They visited some of the spots and restaurants they had gone to while they were in school. Quincy felt like he was finally getting his due.

Quincy and Quinn also went to see Professor Williams. They wanted to surprise the professor. As they walked into his office, Quincy said, "Hey, Professor Williams."

"Hey, Quincy, Quinn. This is a surprise. I wasn't expecting you for another couple of weeks."

"Well, Quincy and I want to celebrate a little bit. Quincy took a tax case. He did so good, that he was paid very handsomely," Quinn said.

"Well, this is cause for a celebration, so we are here to treat you to lunch, Professor, so let's go," Quincy said.

Quincy, Quinn, and the professor went to lunch. They really had a good time catching up.

"So, how long are you two going to be in town?" the professor asked.

"We're leaving on Monday. We haven't really had time to

ourselves since we married, so we are trying to make the best of it," Quincy explained.

After Quincy and Quinn had lunch with the professor, they spent the next few days in Boston, shopping and going to plays, just enjoying each other's company. By the time Monday rolled around, neither one of them wanted to go back home, yet both of them had to get back to their jobs in Kansas City.

Quinn and Quincy touched down at KCI airport. They caught a cab to head home.

As soon as they got through the door, Mary was waiting on them, and she was not very happy. "IT'S ABOUT TIME YOU TWO BROUGHT YOUR BEHINDS HOME."

"Hey Mama!"

"DON'T YOU 'HEY MAMA' ME, QUINCY! LEAVING TOWN WITHOUT LETTING ME KNOW WHERE Y'ALL WERE GOING? THEN ON TOP OF THAT LEAVING ME HERE WITH YOUR CRAZY ASS COUSIN?"

"Well, Mama, we brought you this nice Coach purse, along with a dress, shoes, and a hat to match. Are you still mad at us for leaving you here this past weekend?"

"Well, it depends on how the dress, purse, and shoes look on me."

Quinn and Quincy started laughing at Mary.

***

Quincy was getting settled in after spending a long weekend in Boston with Quinn. Now it was time to get back to work.

While Quincy was working some cases for the court and also some cases for the professor, he got an unexpected guest. James Cantone stopped by Quincy's office. Quincy came out of his office, and to his surprise, James Cantone was waiting in his lobby.

"James, this is a surprise. What brings you down to my part of town?"

"Well, Quincy, I was thinking about how well you did with my tax case. You did such an impressive job. I want to hire you to be my lawyer."

"Sure, James, I would love to be your lawyer."

"OK, Quincy, can you get started this week?"

"Sure, I can start this week, James."

"OK, well, this should get you started!"

James handed Quincy a check for half a million dollars. Quincy looked at James and said, "I haven't done anything yet."

"Well, this is on good faith. I will pay you again when the case is over."

Quincy started to make a lot of money while working for James. For the next couple of years, Quincy's firm started to grow. Quincy was really starting to enjoy his life. His dream was coming true—he was practicing law in his community, taking on more cases within the community. Quincy was able to live the life that he wanted to live.

As Quincy was taking on cases for James, he was making enough money so that Quinn didn't have to work. She could've stayed at home, but Quinn decided to quit being a clerk and went to work with Quincy at his law firm. Quinn was one of the lawyers at the firm.

Quinn was able to work very closely with Quincy, something Quinn dreamed about doing for a long time. Quinn and Quincy wasn't just running a law firm; they were volunteering for the boys and girls' club, putting on programs for kids who were interested in becoming lawyers.

Quincy was really reaping the benefits of working for James Cantone. He went on trips around the world. He moved into a bigger house with his mother and wife.

Quincy became one of the wealthiest lawyers in Kansas City.

He drove through the city, in the neighborhood where he

grew up in, and he would think about all the things that he did as he was growing up. All the fun that he had and all of the sacrifices that his mom and dad made to get him through school. Quincy only wished that his father were here to see what he had accomplished.

***

Quincy was standing out on the balcony of his new office, looking out at the city, reminiscing and thinking about all the things that he went through to get to this point in his life. He said to himself, "I finally did it, I made it in this city. My city!"

CHAPTER 6

I t had been almost two years since Quincy started working for James. Things seemed to be going well for Quincy.

James and his wife had become good friends with Quincy and Quinn. All of the doubts that Quincy had about James were put to bed.

Along with the cases from James and the cases that he was also taking around the city, Quincy's caseload was so full that he had to hire more lawyers to help with the workload.

Quincy's law firm was different from anybody else's. The lawyers that were coming in would get a chance to work on some of the cases that Quincy had brought in. They were paid a certain salary for working on them. Yet they could keep all of the profits from the cases that they brought in themselves.

Quincy was also still taking cases from his professor, at least two every month. It wasn't that Quincy was greedy or anything. Taking cases from Professor Williams gave Quincy a chance to get out of town at least once or twice a month.

Everything was going well for Quincy, until one night he got a strange phone call.

"Hello!" Quincy said, half sleep.

"Hello, is this Quincy Black?"

"Yes, this is Quincy!"

"My name is Seeley Brown. I work for James Cantone, and he told me to call you if I ever had a problem, so that's what I'm doing. I'm calling you."

"Mr. Brown, do you know what time it is?"

"Yes I do, it is three in the morning. I will meet you at your office in about thirty minutes." Then Seeley hung up the phone.

"Quincy, who was that on the phone?" Quinn asked.

"I guess it was one of James's friends or employees. They want me to meet them at the office."

"AT THREE O'CLOCK IN THE MORNING? QUINCY!"

"I know, Quinn, I will be careful."

Quincy got up and headed down to his office. Just as soon as Quincy was getting ready to unlock the door, Seeley was knocking on the window. Quincy opened the door and they went in the back.

"So, Seeley, is it? OK. What kind of problem do you have, where you have to call me at three o'clock in the morning?"

"Look, Mr. Black, James Cantone told me that you are the best at what you do. So I have a major problem that I need your help with. I shot a cop about three hours ago."

"YOU DID WHAT, MR. BROWN?" Quincy asked.

"I shot a cop."

"Mr. Brown, I don't handle cases like that for James."

"Well, it looks like you are now, because this was the number I was given by James to call in case something like this was to ever happen. SO YOU NEED TO FIX IT! There are seven hundred thousand dollars in this bag. That should be enough for the fee and trial."

"LOOK, SEELEY, MAYBE YOU DIDN'T HEAR WHAT I SAID! I'M NOT TAKING YOUR CASE!"

"LOOK HERE, YOU DUMBASS NIGGA! YOU ARE GOING TO

TAKE THIS CASE, OR THERE WILL BE PROBLEMS."

"MR. BROWN, YOU NEED TO LEAVE BEFORE I THROW YOUR ASS OUT OF MY OFFICE!"

"You really don't have the slightest idea who you're dealing with, do you? I am a hit man, and I work for a very powerful man in this city!"

"I don't care if you work for the president himself! I'm still not taking this case."

"We will see about that, Quincy! We will finish talking about this tomorrow. Keep the money, because one way or another you *will* take this case."

After Seeley had left Quincy's office, Quincy started to wonder who James Cantone really was.

Quincy went home to try to get some sleep, but he couldn't; he kept wondering about who he was involved with. It was six thirty in the morning when Quincy went ahead and got on up. He got ready and headed down to the office.

Quinn got up around nine thirty, and noticed that Quincy was already gone. When she got to the office, she noticed that Quincy was already there.

"Hey Quincy, sweetie, did you come home at all last night?"

"Yes I did, but left right back out at six thirty."

"Is everything okay?"

"Yes, Quinn, everything is okay. James should be coming in shortly, so can you can let Janet know to send him on back?"

"OK, Quincy! Are you sure everything is OK?"

"Yes, Quinn, I'm fine." He kissed Quinn on the cheek.

Just as Quinn was leaving Quincy's office, James and Seeley came in. Janet sent them back into Quincy's office.

"Hey, James, Seeley."

"Hey, Quincy, I am so sorry about his morning! Seeley was not supposed to call you. We have other lawyers that deal with this kind of mess."

"No problem, James, here is your money back."

"Quincy, can you please do me a huge favor? I know that you don't deal with this type of case, but just this once can you take his case for me? Keep the seven hundred thousand dollars, and after the case I will pay you twenty million. You already know the case."

"James, you know I don't take cases like these."

"Quincy, just this once can you please take it? I promise this is the only time you would have to deal with this kind of case."

"OK, James, I will take the case. When is Seeley turning himself in?" Quinn asked.

"He'll go turn himself in right after we leave your office."

"OK, James, I will get started on the case right away."

After James and Seeley left Quincy's office, James slapped Seely.

"WHAT IN THE HELL IS WRONG WITH YOU? YOU CALLED THE WRONG LAWYER! I WAS TRYING TO KEEP QUINCY AWAY FROM THAT SIDE OF THE BUSINESS. IF I DIDN'T NEED YOU RIGHT NOW, I WOULD KILL YOU!"

Seely turned himself in. Quincy started his defense so he could get Seely clear of these charges.

Quincy cleared all of his appointments and pushed them back for two weeks so he could work on Seeley's case. He looked at and studied every inch of this case, trying to find a loophole.

Quincy called for another meeting between the DA, the judge, and Seeley. Judge Wallace was kind of getting tired of meeting like this.

"OK, gentlemen. Mr. Black, I assume that you have a very good reason for this meeting."

"As usual, I do, Your Honor!"

"DON'T GET CUTE, MR. BLACK!"

"Sorry, Your Honor! I'm here to put in a request to have the charges dropped for my client."

"Mr. Black, you realize that your client is facing murder charges, right?"

"I do realize that, but if your officer had done his job right, then we would not be having this conversation. Your arresting officer did not read my client his rights."

"So you mean to tell me that one of our finest did not read a murder suspect his rights? Mr. Wright, did you know about this?"

"No I didn't, Your Honor!"

"So you do realize that the charges will have to be dropped, right, Mr. Wright?"

"Yes, Your Honor, I do realize that!"

"Well, Mr. Black, since you brought this to our attention, all of the charges will be dropped against your client. You are free to go, Mr. Brown."

"That's it? I only spent two weeks in jail and now I'm free to go? Damn, James was right, Quincy, you *are* good!"

"What, you had doubts, Seeley?"

"Wow! You guys done all ready?" James asked as he met them outside the courthouse.

"Yeah, James, you should have been there. Quincy is really good. I thought you were joking."

"Thanks for taking this case for me!"

"No problem, James! Hey, can we talk for a moment?"

"Well, of course, Quincy! Ah, yeah, by the way, here is your check before I forget."

"Thanks, James!"

"No, thank you, Quincy! You earned every penny considering the circumstances."

"James, I have to be honest with you. I really appreciate everything that you have done for me and my family. It means a lot to me, that you gave me a chance when no one else would. But I'm going to have to end our business relationship."

"REALLY? WHY, YOU UNGRATEFUL BASTARD. ME AND MY ORGANIZATION HAVE MADE YOU THE RICHEST BLACK LAWYER IN KANSAS CITY. THIS IS HOW YOU TREAT US? TREAT ME?! LET ME TELL WHAT'S GOING TO HAPPEN: YOU ARE GOING TO KEEP WORKING FOR ME. YOU ARE GOING TO TAKE ANY CASE I GIVE YOU. MAKE SOME MONEY, BE HAPPY. IF YOU DON'T, AND IF YOU REFUSE, I WILL KILL YOUR WIFE AND YOUR MOTHER."

Quincy looked at James and said, "So, are you threatening me?"

"Yes, Quincy, I am. If you don't believe me, just try me!"

CHAPTER 7

Ever since Quincy had that meeting with James, that was all he could think about. It had been three to four months since Quincy had the meeting with James. Quincy was taking every case that James and his associates brought him. He was trying to figure out a way to get out from under James's thumb. So Quincy cleared his schedule for a couple of weeks. He was going to Boston to try to find some information on James. Something he could use to get out from under him.

He told Quinn what was going on. Quinn decided to go with Quincy to Boston. Since James threatened to kill Mary and Quinn, they took Mary with them to Boston for a couple weeks with them. Quincy called and told Professor Williams that he was on his way to Boston.

When Quincy arrived in Boston, Professor Williams met Quincy, Quinn, and Mary at the airport to pick them up. While Quinn and Mary did a little shopping and sightseeing, Quincy and Professor Williams headed back to his office to discuss what was going on.

"So, Quincy, what is going on?"

"Do you know a guy by the name of James Cantone?"

"James Cantone? Yes, I know him very well. Quincy, how do you know James?"

"Well, I am his lawyer! That's the client Quinn and I were talking about the last time we were here. I'm trying to get out from under his thumb."

"Quincy, I was afraid you were going to say that. What happened, did he threaten you?"

"Yes he did, Professor Williams. That's why Mama and Quinn are with me. James doesn't know that I left town."

"QUINCY! Why didn't you come to me about James?"

"Well, Professor, I really wasn't thinking, and I didn't think that you could do anything."

"Quincy, you really should never underestimate me. James Cantone is the third generation of Mafia. His father and grandfather were very well known throughout the world. For the past twenty years, James has been making a name for himself. Yet, about ten years ago, James killed the wrong person. James killed a judge, but this wasn't just any judge. This judge had ties to other Mafia family members. That would have put James in a troublesome position if he had stayed here in Massachusetts. He would have ended up in jail or dead. So they made a deal with him, to leave Boston and never come back.

"For the last ten years he has been setting up shop in Kansas City, Missouri. James has family there. I heard that the DA had some good proof that he wasn't paying his taxes. If that were true, he would go away for at least ten to twenty years. From what I heard, it was at least seven years of not paying his taxes. Yet he got cleared of the charges."

"Yeah he did, Professor Williams. That was me, that was my first case for James. We didn't even have a trial. I proved that the documents were legit. The DA had been holding up the case for at least two years. So when I showed the judge all of the time and resources that had been wasted, plus how real the documents were, the charges were dropped and the case was dismissed. James was so impressed that he hired me to be his lawyer, and I was also the lawyer for most of his colleagues.

"I'm not going to lie, Professor Williams, the money was really good. Things were going really well. I actually thought that James was a legitimate businessman. On paper and under certain circumstances, he is. That all changed when one of his top hit men called me at three in the morning. He told me that James told him to call me in case of an emergency. Yet he called the wrong lawyer.

"Seeley had shot somebody that night. He met me at my office and threw me a bag that had seven hundred thousand dollars in it. When I told Seeley that I was not going to take the case, that's when I found out who James was. Seeley tried to threaten me, but I told him to get out of my office. After I told him that, I knew that he would be back the next day with James.

"Sure enough, at around nine in the morning, here come James and Seeley. I told James that I don't usually take cases like that. Yet he begged me to do it; he even told me to keep the seven hundred thousand dollars and that he would pay me twenty million dollars if I took the case. I took it, had the charges dropped without Seeley even going to trial.

"After the meeting with the DA and the judge, I had a meeting with James. I told him that I could not continue our business relationship. He wasn't too happy with that. He called me an ungrateful bastard, then he said this was what was going to happen. He told me that I was going to take whatever case he or his friends gave me, and make some money. Basically, do what he said to do, keep my mouth shut and make money while I was doing it. If I didn't, he was going to kill Mama and Quinn. That's what I have been doing for the last two mouths. The first chance I got to leave for a vacation, I took it. That's why I came here, Professor. I have to find a way to get out from under James's thumb. I can't put my family through this. I haven't even told my mother what is going on."

"Well, Quincy, I might be able to help you. I was kind of in the same circumstances years ago with James's grandfather. I built up some information on the entire family, going all the way back to the beginning of their family. I told you that James was the third generation of the Mafia family. Actually, he is like the tenth generation. There are a lot things that his family have done that are not on record."

"Professor Williams, how did get from out from under James's grandfather's thumb?"

"What I'm about to tell you, you can't tell anyone else. I am James's uncle! His grandfather had an affair with my mother while he was married. When my mother got pregnant, James Sr. was pissed. He really didn't know what to do. If his wife had found out, all hell would have broken lose. So he moved me and my mother away from Massachusetts. He moved us to New Jersey, so no one would know who I was. I was staying in a quiet, small, suburban neighborhood.

"He supported us while I was in grade school, high school, and college. I got my Undergrad at NYU. Yet I wanted to go to Harvard Law. At first, my father said no. Yet my mother changed his mind. As mean and stubborn as he was, my mother could soften his heart and get him to do anything.

"After I graduated from Harvard Law and became a lawyer, he wanted me to come and work with him. That's what I did, yet I started noticing the things that my father was doing. The drugs, prostitution, gunrunning and human trafficking. I went to confront him about all of this. He said to me, 'BOY, HOW DO YOU THINK I TOOK CARE OF YOU? ALL OF THIS PAID FOR YOUR SCHOOL.'

"I told him it was wrong. We got into a huge fight about it. My father told me that if I wanted to stay here and work for him, that I better shut my mouth and get with the program. That's what I did.

"Being a lawyer gave me access to a lot of information. I was able to pull up all of the cases that they tried to nail my father for. The file went back for at least thirty years.

I did my homework, I took these case files and gave them to the DA. The files that I had on my father and the case the DA was trying to build against my father would end up sending my father to jail for at least twenty years. Before I made a deal, I made sure they got my mother out of the country. I had them fake my death. I changed my name to my mother's maiden name. Since no one but my father knew who I was, it was very, very easy to bring him down.

"Now, my brother took over where my father left off. He passed the business to my nephew, James. I have been collecting and gathering info on my brother and my nephew. I also have info on the Organization as well. This type of information, if it ever got out, could leave them behind bars for the rest of their lives. Or it could get them killed.

"Quincy, you also should go get some information on James from the DA, but be careful with this information. This is very dangerous!"

CHAPTER 8

Q uincy had received a lot of information on James. He was very surprised to know that Professor Williams was related to James. Nevertheless, after the meeting with Professor Williams, Quincy and Professor Williams met up with Quinn and Mary. All four of them enjoyed each other's company.

Quincy had gotten the information that he needed. He was going to use it to get out from under James's thumb. Quincy had enough information to send James and the rest of the Organization to jail. Even worse, all of this information could get James killed.

Quincy had to make sure that his mother was safe. He talked his mother into staying in Massachusetts with Professor Williams. Mary had not been out of town since Quincy's graduation. Quincy thought that it would do Mary some good to spend some time out of town for a while.

Quincy wanted Quinn to stay there with Mary, but Quinn was not going to leave Quincy's side, so Quincy and Quinn headed back to Kansas City.

When Quincy got to the house, he had at least twenty messages. All the messages were from James or someone in the Organization.

Quincy started going through his messages and returning calls. While Quincy and Quinn were working, trying to get caught up, James and Seeley walked into the office. Quincy immediately got off the phone.

"Hey, James, Seeley, what brings you two down here?"

"We have been wondering where you have been."

"My mother and Quinn wanted to go out of town for a little bit. Since I have been working a lot of hours lately, I decided to take some time off."

"Well, Quincy, the next time you decide to take some time off, can you please let us know? We have a lot work to do, and you taking two weeks off put us behind big time."

"James, I thought you had other lawyers besides me?"

"We do, Quincy, but none of them are as good as you! So please can you just give us a heads-up next time?"

"Sure, James, I will keep that in mind."

"Seeley, can you give Quincy and I a couple of minutes?"

Seeley nodded and left the office.

"Look, Quincy, I know we have had our differences, but like it or not you are the lawyer of a very large organization."

"Don't you mean I'm a lawyer for the Mafia?

"Well, call it whatever you like! You still work for us. THE NEXT TIME YOUR BLACK ASS LEAVES TOWN WITHOUT LETTING ME KNOW, I DON'T CARE IF IT'S AT YOUR MOTHER'S FUNERAL, I WILL SEND SEELEY TO BRING YOUR BLACK ASS BACK HERE TO KANSAS CITY. DO YOU UNDERSTAND ME, QUINCY?!"

"YES, JAMES, I UNDERSTAND! Now, do you mind? I have a lot of work to catch up on!"

***

Quincy did have a lot of work to catch up on. Most of the cases that everybody was calling in for were simple. They called in for Quincy, but he would send one of his associates. Yet he would call the client and tell him what was going on. How the case should go. Quincy also told them that he was sending his associates to court with them due to the fact that he had a very heavy caseload. Just about all of the Organization understood, and their cases were dismissed. James was kind of pissed, but as the cases got dismissed and went in their favor, he was relieved.

Quincy knew that he had to get away from James or make him go away. So as Quincy got his caseload worked down, he started to look into how to get out from underneath James's thumb.

Quincy called for a meeting with the whole Mafia Organization. Not James, but all of the families. James was wondering why Quincy wanted to meet with everybody. Quincy told him that he wanted to go over how they could bring in a little more money than usual. James liked that, so he went along with the meeting.

As the whole Organization came to the meeting and was sitting down, Quincy came in and started passing out workbooks to each of the families' leaders. Everybody thought that this meeting was about how to make more profit. Instead of making more profits, they were about to make a leadership change.

"Good evening, gentlemen, I know that it is late, so let's get right to it. In front of you are some workbooks. I know that everybody thinks that this is about making more money. If you open your workbooks, you will realize that it's not. The workbook in front of you has everybody's individual cases that go back at least thirty years. Everything, everybody that you killed, every bribe that was made, every crooked deal that everybody has ever done is in these workbooks.

"Now, this is how things are going to go from now on. I will now be in charge of all of the Organization. If anybody says no or disagrees with me on this arrangement, all of this information will be sent to the district attorney's office here in Kansas City and the US District Attorney as well. Now, does anyone have any questions?"

"WHY, YOU DUMBASS NIGGA! DO YOU THINK THAT WE ARE GOING LET YOU GET AWAY WITH THIS? I SHOULD HAVE GOT-

TEN RID OF YOUR BLACK ASS WHEN I HAD A CHANCE!"

As James was screaming at Quincy, Seeley pulled a gun out on James. "James, sit down, and stop being so disrespectful. Quincy is not done talking yet."

"Oh yeah, if anybody tries to threaten me or my family, all of this information will automatically be sent to the US District Attorney."

"Quincy, why are you doing this? Do you really think that you are going to get away with this?"

"Yes, James, I *am* going to get away this! The reason why is because YOU PISSED OFF THE WRONG DAMN NIGGA! Now, if you gentlemen don't mind, my wife wants me home early tonight. So please take some time to think things over. We will met again in a couple of weeks."

CHAPTER 9

It had been about a month since Quincy had a meeting with all of the families of the Organization. Quincy hold told them they would meet in two weeks, yet Quincy went ahead and gave them a month to let things sink in.

It really was a shock to James to see Seeley was now working with Quincy. Quincy and Seeley would meet just about every day, going over details on how to grow the business, how to make even more money. They also knew that there would be some blowback because of the new leadership. They knew that James was not going to go for Quincy taking his place.

Seeley had gotten word that James had put out a hit on Quincy and his whole family. Quincy's mother was already out of town. Quinn didn't want to go; she wanted to stay with Quincy. Quincy finally convinced her to go to Massachusetts with his mother and Professor Williams. He wanted to make sure that Quinn and his mother were safe. He knew that things were about to get very messy.

Quincy and Seeley set up a meeting with the Organization. Everybody came to the meeting—everybody except James. So Seeley went and got James, brought him to the meeting in his robe.

"WHAT THE HELL ARE YOU DOING, COMING TO GET ME LIKE THIS?"

"Well, James, did you know that we had a meeting?"

"Yes, Quincy, I knew that we had a meeting! I just wasn't going to come!"

"Really, James? Why wouldn't you want to come to your own organization's meeting?"

"You little sh— Are you really going to ask me that?"

"Could it be because you put a hit on me and my family?"

"I SURE DID PUT A HIT OUT ON YOUR BLACK ASS AND MONKEY."

"So, James, you hired these men to kill me and my family, right?"

Seeley brought the hit men into the room, all beaten and halfway dead.

"Now, this is a lesson for everyone in here. This is what happens when you try to kill me or my family."

Seeley brought James's family into the room.

"QUINCY, WHAT THE HELL ARE YOU DOING?" James screamed as Seeley threw James's daughter and wife to the floor. Seeley took out his gun and handed it to Quincy. Quincy shot both James's wife and his daughter in front of him.

"YOU BASTARD, I AM GOING TO KILL YOU FOR THIS!!" James screamed.

Quincy took a match and some lighter fluid, poured the fluid on James, and set him on fire in front of everybody. James started to scream as he was burned alive. Seeley couldn't take the screaming anymore, so he shot James in the head to put him out of his misery.

Everybody that was sitting at that table was starting to realize that Quincy was going to be a force to be reckoned with.

"Quincy, was it wise to kill James? Now that you have killed him, it is a possibility that you could have created a bigger mess,"

Alan, a Mafia member, said.

"Alan, are you talking about his cousin in Boston? Jarred?"

"Yes, Quincy, Jarred! Jarred is crazier than James was. Once he finds out that James is dead, he is going to tear Kansas City up until he finds you."

"Well, I think I might have a way to deal with Jarred," Quincy said.

Quincy told the rest of the Organization to lay low for a while. He had to fly back to Boston to check on his mother and Quinn.

Quinn and Quincy had bought a condo and house outside of Boston. When Quincy arrived in Boston, he headed to the condo. When he got there, Professor Williams, Quinn, and his mother were having dinner. His mother was enjoying her time there with the professor. Quinn and the professor looked at Quincy's face and wondered what was going on.

"Mama, can you stay here for a little bit? The professor and I have to help Quincy with something. We will be right back," Quincy said.

All three of them headed to the other room.

"Okay, Quincy, what's going on? When can Mama and I come back home?"

"Not yet, Quinn!"

"What do mean, not yet?"

"Well, we might have another problem. James's cousin, Jarred, might be coming to Kansas City. Once word gets back to him that James is dead—"

"QUINCY! WHAT DO YOU MEAN, JAMES IS DEAD?" Quinn yelled.

"I will give you two a couple of minutes," the professor said as he walked out of the room.

"Quincy, why is James dead?"

"Because I killed him! I had to. Even if James had been sent to jail, he still would have found a way to kill all of us. Quinn, he already had hit men in place to kill you and Mama!"

"OK, Quincy, so what about this Jarred?"

"I came back to Boston to see if I could make friends with James's enemies. If I can do that, and make a deal with them, with them on our side, then we will have a chance against Jarred when he comes knocking."

Quincy had gone and found some enemies of James and Jared. In fact, he found a lot of their enemies.

Quincy had a hush meeting with them in Boston, trying to make a deal with the other families in Boston. These families were not fans of James or his family. Quincy wasn't any better, considering that Quincy was black. Yet with Seeley there with Quincy, he helped them see that Quincy would be a major ally.

Once Quincy and Seeley told the others that they had killed James, well, that kind of information got the Calhoun family very interested. So Quincy was able to make a deal with the Calhoun family that was in Boston. Quincy was also able to get some more muscle for when Jarred tried to come seek revenge for the death of James.

After the meeting that Quincy and Seeley had with the Calhoun family, Seeley headed back to Kansas City to make sure things were put in place, and also to prepare for Jarred. Seeley thought that there could be a chance that Jarred might not show up, yet Quincy knew better.

Quincy stayed in Boston for a few more days. He wanted to spend time with Quinn and his mother before he headed back to Kansas City.

Quinn and Quincy went to dinner. Quinn wanted some quality time with Quincy, and she also wanted to know what was going on as well.

"Quincy, please tell me what's going on. How did the meeting go?"

"Well, at first they didn't want to deal with me because of my color, although they didn't come out and say it. You can tell, though. But once they found out that James was dead, it was a totally different ball game after that. They were more than willing to help us! When I offered to give them James's whole territory in Boston and Kansas City, they jumped on it. They really can't stand James or his family.

"So after we set terms and made a deal, Seeley went back to Kansas City to prepare, just in case Jarred goes there."

"Quincy, do you think he is going to go to Kansas City?"

"Jared and James grew up together; they were like brothers. So yes, Quinn, I do. That's why I need you and mama to stay here for a while."

"At least this is over with! Okay, Quincy, we will stay here until it's safe to come back home. But please come back to me!"

"I will, Quinn."

CHAPTER 10

Quincy finally headed back to Kansas City. He met up with Seeley to go over some business details. But before they could go over anything, Seeley had some very bad news to tell him.

"Seeley, what's wrong? Why do you look like that?"

"Jarred had someone shoot up your house. He is also on his way here."

"Well, we figured that, right, Seeley?"

"Yes we did, but I'm just glad that we got your mother and Quinn out of town before the house was hit."

"Well, Seeley, let's come up with a plan to send this jackass back home."

Quincy and Seeley worked on coming up with a plan to put an end to Jarred once and for all. After Jarred had Quincy's house shot up, Quincy knew that it was just a matter of time before Jarred showed up.

When Jarred arrived at Kansas City, he starting torturing and killing people, trying to find out where Quincy was. Quincy and Seeley left bread crumbs for Jarred to follow. The bread crumbs led all the way back to where Quincy was. Quincy knew that Jarred would be coming for him.

***

Quincy and Seeley were at a bar in in the West Bottoms. Quincy had the whole place surrounded, yet you couldn't tell.

Jarred finally arrived at the bar where Quincy was. He went into the bar with about twelve men deep. He left twelve men outside, surrounding the whole bar.

"Well, finally we meet. I have been looking for you all over Kansas City, Mr. Quincy Black. I figured your black nigger ass would be down here with the rest of the trash."

"Jarred Cantone, how the hell have you been?"

"Well, Quincy, I heard through the grapevine that you are trying to take over the Organization. I also heard that you killed my cousin and his family."

"Well, Jarred, you have heard a lot, haven't you? Yes, everything that you have heard is true!"

"QUINCY, YOU DUMBASS NIGGA! WHY DID YOU KILL MY COUSIN, AFTER EVERYTHING HE DID FOR YOU?!"

"Your cousin threatened my family! That's something that you just don't do! On top of that, I heard you just shot up my house!"

"I'm tired of playing games with you! I TOLD MY COUSIN THAT HE SHOULD HAVE KILLED YOUR BLACK ASS A LONG TIME AGO."

"Yep, Jarred, maybe James should have killed me when he had the chance. Since he didn't, I'm going to give you something that I never gave him! I'm going to give you three options: You stay here and try to kill me, or you go home and get your family, then leave this country and turn over your business over to me."

"What's the third option, Quincy?"

"You can stay here and watch me dismember your wife and kids. It's your choice. By the way, here are some pictures of your wife and kids, if you're having any doubts."

"YOU LITTLE B—"

Just as Jarred started to scream at Quincy, Jarred pulled his gun out. Seeley pulled his and shot Jarred in the hand. That started a chain reaction. All of Quincy's men took out Jarred's men inside the bar and outside of it. It happened so fast, it was like a domino effect.

Jarred got up, holding his hand. It was bleeding pretty bad.

"Now, Jared, that offer still stands. Do you want to live, or die?"

"QUINCY, MARK MY WORDS—"

"I'M TIRED OF ALL THE THREATS!" Quincy pulled out his gun and put it in Jarred's mouth. "Now, I'm going to ask you one last time: do you want to live, or die? You have five seconds to answer me."

Quincy started counting: ONE... TWO... THREE... FOUR... He pulled back the lever on the gun.

"OK, OK... Stop... I will leave... I will leave the country," Jarred mumbled with the gun in his mouth.

"Seeley will make sure that you get to the airport in one piece. You have five days to pack and sign over all of your assets to me and get the hell out of the country. Now take your Italian wobbly ass on and get the f*** out of my city.

"Oh yeah, by the way, Jarred, the Calhouns told me to tell you hi."

Quincy and Jarred had the Calhoun family watch Jarred to make sure he got his things in order, and also to make sure Jarred left the country when his five days were up. Within the third day, Jarred had transferred all his assets over to Quincy. During the next few days, Jarred and his family booked a flight out of the country.

Quincy waited for another month to make sure that it was safe before he brought Quinn and his mother back home. In the meantime, Quincy set a meeting with the rest of the Organization. Quincy and Seeley had come up with a plan where everybody could make a lot of money. Quincy's plan would increase profits for all the families by at least one thousand percent. Within the next fifteen to twenty years, everybody in the organization would become billionaires. When James was in charge, the most that anyone ever made was three hundred to four hundred million dollars. But for every head of the family to become billionaires? That idea right there seemed to make them forget that Quincy was black.

Of course, the leader of one of the families, Larry, asked Quincy a question.

"Quincy, that all sounds really good, but it just sounds like a fool's dream. Just how are we going to become billionaires?"

"Well, Larry, my friend, we are going to start selling drugs."

"We have never gotten involved with drugs, and we never will."

"Larry, if we can control who we sell drugs to and where we sell them, we can control the outcome and make as much money as we want. We need to start selling outside the country first. Then we bring it inside of the country. Certain areas, and not where we stay at. If we do this right, for the next fifteen to twenty, maybe in ten, we all can make a lot of money. Nobody is selling this type of drug yet. If everybody in here would trust me, look beyond the color of my skin, we can become very, very rich!"

CHAPTER 11

It had been about nine months since all of the chaos went down with Jarred. The neighborhood was a lot more quieter. Quincy had just finished fixing up the house.

Quinn was so happy to be home; she was even more glad that all of the drama was over. Mary was back in Massachusetts with Professor Williams; they were getting pretty close. Plus, she was finally starting to enjoy her life. Everything was coming together.

As for the plan that Quincy had put into motion for the Organization, they were starting to see profits from it already. All of the families were starting to bring in at least forty more percent than last year. Quincy's idea of keeping the drugs in certain neighborhoods was working so far.

Quincy thought if he took over the Mafia, that he could keep the neighborhood safe. He was still trying to set up workshops for kids that wanted to go to colleges. Quincy and Quinn were also trying to help out low-income families. He was trying to keep his community safe from all of the chaos, crime, and prostitution. Yet all of the money and power was going to Quincy's head. Quincy figure that he could run Kansas City. He would be a lawyer by daytime and a Mafia boss by night.

Quinn knew what Quincy was doing. She didn't know all of the details, but she knew. She didn't like it much nor did she ask any questions. Quinn always referred to it as "Quincy's other business."

Regardless of Quincy's other business, his relationship with Quinn was stronger. Even he and Seeley became pretty close.

Business was doing so well that Quincy and Seeley decided to throw a little party downtown, but they would have a meeting first.

"Seeley, is everybody here for the meeting?"

"Yes, Quincy, everybody is here."

"Quincy, I thought we were here for a party, not a business meeting."

"We *are* here for a party Larry, I just wanted to gather you in here for a toast. This year is almost over. I know that we have had a rough one, yet all of that is behind us. I'm proud to say that we are ahead of schedule. We are already making one hundred percent more than what we were last year."

Just soon as Quincy said that, everyone started to clap out of amazement.

"So, gentlemen, let's celebrate, get drunk, have a good time with your ladies. Please enjoy your night," Quincy finished with a toast.

As everybody was at the party enjoying themselves, Quincy and Seeley were having their own little meeting.

"So, Seeley, this is for you!" Quincy gave Seely a check for fifty million dollars. "I told you, Seeley, you're not a hit man anymore. I told you we're partners in this thing. We are all going to be billionaires, not just me or the heads of the families. You are included in that. I wouldn't be in this position if it weren't for you. So thank you, Seeley!"

"No, thank *you*, Quincy! James would have never done anything like this for me. I really appreciate it!"

"You're welcome! Is there anybody that we have to worry about yet?"

"Well, Quincy, I would keep my eye on Larry. Larry still doesn't like the fact that you are head of the Organization. Mainly because you are black."

"Yeah, I figured as much."

"Quincy, if your projections are right, in the next five to ten years we should all be billionaires. As long as the money keeps coming in, Larry won't say anything. Eventually, Larry is going to want to take over the Organization, especially from a black man, no matter how much money you have made for him. It's all about power with Larry."

"Well, we better watch him, then. How are the other parts of the business doing?"

"Everything else is running smoothly. Even the Calhoun family is satisfied with their return."

While Quincy and Seeley were still talking, there was a knock on the door. It was Quinn.

"May I come in, boys? I know that you two are discussing business, but this is supposed to be a party. Seeley, I do believe that there is a beautiful lady waiting to dance with you," Quinn said as she laughed.

"Well, Quincy, on that note, I will talk to you later."

"OK, Seeley."

"So, Mr. Black, what do you want to do for the rest of the night?"

"Well, Mrs. Black, I don't care what we do, just as long as we are together." As they kissed, Quincy hesitantly pushed him away for a second and said, "Before the night gets late, I have something to tell you."

"Is it bad?"

"No, Quincy, it's actually good news for a change."

"Well, what is it?"

"I'm pregnant!"

"WHAT DID YOU SAY?"

"Quincy, you heard me! I'm pregnant."

Quincy was so happy that he picked Quinn up and swung her around.

"Oh, Quinn, baby, I'm so sorry. I didn't mean to pick you up."

"Quincy, sweetie, it's OK!" Quinn said, laughing. "So, Mr. Black, I'm about to go upstairs to our room. Do you care to join me?"

"Sure, sweetie, I will be right there."

As Quinn kissed Quincy, Quincy kind of wanted to savor the moment. He was about to become a father. Right then Quincy got this crazy idea that if he ever had two sons, that they would help him run Kansas City. They would be a force to be reckoned with. That right there would be a family dynasty!

CHAPTER 12

I t had been about twenty years, and a lot of things had changed over the years in Kansas City. Yet some things had stayed the same. Quincy was still head over the Mafia. Quincy also had two sons: Jackson Black, who went by Jax for short, and Quincy Black Jr.

Quincy had projected that the whole Organization would become billionaires within twenty years. What Quincy projected and predicted had come true. Every head of the Mafia family within the Organization had made at least a billion dollars. Things were looking up for Quincy.

The only problem was the way the Organization made the money. When Quincy had brought up the idea of selling drugs, he proposed that it would not be sold in their city, yet slowly but surely the drugs finally reached the neighborhoods. Quincy had gotten to the point where he just didn't give a damn as long as he was making money.

Now that his two boys were growing up—Jax was sixteen and Quincy Jr. fourteen—his dream would finally come true. Quincy had known that one day he and his two sons would run Kansas City, Missouri. He was going to do everything in his power to make sure that dream came true.

Quincy had the boys run errands for him. Well, he had Jax running an errand for him.

"Jax, where are we going?"

"Q, you didn't have to come. I told you that I had to go do something for Daddy!"

"Well, damn, Jax, how long is this going to take? I wanted to stop by Iesha's house."

"Quincy Junior, the only reason you want to stop by my girl-friend's house is so you can see her friend that's been staying over there. Negro, you are not slick!" Jax was laughing. "We are almost at Daddy's office. As soon as I go in and drop this package off, we will head over to Iesha's house."

***

"Seeley, I wanted to run something by you before the meeting."

"What's that, Quincy?"

"Well, Seeley, I have been thinking about bringing the boys into the fold."

"Well, that sounds like a good idea. The only thing that concerns me is Q. Quincy, I love my nephew to death, yet Q can be a hothead. I'm afraid that one day he could say something that could get him killed. Now, on the other hand, Jax is very low key and very smart . He might be smarter than you, Quincy!"

"WOW! Seeley, if I didn't know any better, I would think you were trying to replace me with Jax." Both of them laughed. "Let's have a talk with both of them this weekend, then we will have them sit in on our next meeting."

"Ah yeah, speaking of the meeting, your favorite person will not be able to make it again."

"Don't tell me, Seeley. Larry, huh?"

"Yes, sir!"

"So, did Larry give an explanation as to why he can't make it this time?"

"All he said was that it was a family emergency."

"What have you found out about our sneaky little friend?"

"Well, Quincy, I found out that he is trying to organize a takeout. He's been having small secret meetings with a few of the families. He is trying to prove that you are incompetent, and the fact that you are a black man, that doesn't help matters much."

"After all the money we made together. We are all billionaires and he still doesn't like me, huh? Why can't we all just get along?

"OK, whatever! Seeley, you know what to do."

"It's already in motion, Quincy!"

"OK, good! Now where in hell are those two knucklehead sons of mine?"

Just as soon as Quincy said that, Jax was pulling up.

"Hey Dad, hey Uncle Seeley."

"Jax, Son, what took you so long to get here?"

"Well, Daddy, your son wanted to stop and get something to eat. I would have been here earlier if somebody hadn't been bitching about being hungry."

"Jax, watch your mouth. Next week, I want both of you to meet me back here at the office. Q, make sure you eat first, OK? I will see you boys at home later on, right?"

"OK, Daddy!"

As Jax and Q were on their way to Jax's girlfriend's house, sirens started going off.

"Oh crap, what is it, Jax? What the hell are we being pulled over for?"

"Q, calm down, and please let me handle this."

The officer pulled over Jax and Quincy. He got out of the car and walked up on the driver's side where Jax was.

"Is there a problem, Officer?"

"Can I see your license and registration, please?"

"HEY DUDE, MY BROTHER ASKED YOU IF THERE WAS A PROBLEM!"

"Q, I told that I got this!" Jax handed the officer his license and registration. The officer went back to his car to check and to make sure that they were legit, but he came back and said, "Can you two please step out of the car?"

"I'M NOT STEPPING OUT OF THIS CAR UNTIL YOU TELL US WHY YOU PULLED US OVER. YOU MUST NOT KNOW WHO MY FATHER IS!"

"QUINCY JUNIOR, WOULD YOU PLEASE SHUT THE HELL UP AND LET ME HANDLE THIS?! Officer, can you tell us why you pulled us over and why you are arresting us?"

"We had a couple of Mercedes Benz stolen from the car lot."

"Well, Officer, this car that we are riding in was just shipped from overseas. This car is not even on the market yet."

"Nevertheless, Mr. Black, I will still have to take you and your brother in."

"Sir, you do realize who my father is, right?"

"Yes, Mr. Black, I do know who your father is!"

"OK, Officer Stanley—I hope that's OK that I call you that. Let me tell you what's going to happen if you arrest us. The judge will take one look at this case and ask you if you are a fool. Just like I told you, the car that you have accused me and brother of stealing is not even on the market yet. Therefore, the dealerships have not even received them yet. They won't receive them until the beginning of next year. Then you, my friend, well, you will be charged with racial discrimination and harassment. You will be suspended pending an investigation. All the charges filed against my brother and I will be dropped."

The police was getting very irritated and pissed off, mostly because he knew everything that Jax told him was probably right, so he went ahead and arrested Jax and Q anyway.

When word got back to Quincy about his boys being arrested and the reason why they were arrested, Quincy was not too happy.

Quincy and Seeley went down to the police department where the boys were being held at. When Quincy walked into the police department, everyone stopped and spoke to Quincy. Every police officer knew Quincy. All except Officer Stanley, who thought he knew who Quincy was.

Quincy went up to the front desk.

"Well, hello, Judge Black, can I help you?"

"Can you explain to me how someone can be arrested for stealing a car that's not even on the market yet? A car that none of the lots have or will have for the next twelve months?"

"Well, Judge Black, that doesn't make any sense."

"Son, I'm glad that I'm not the only one that sees that. Can you get your chief of police down here?"

"Well, Judge Black, I think he's in bed."

"SON, I DON'T CARE IF HE'S IN BED WITH TEN HOOKERS. YOU BETTER GET HIS ASS IN HERE, RIGHT NOW!"

The officer that was attending the desk hurried up and called the chief of police, and told him what was going on. The chief of police rushed down to the police station and pulled Quincy and Seeley into his office.

"So, Chief, can you explain this to me?"

"Judge Black, I don't understand it myself. I am having your boys released as we speak."

"Well, I would really appreciate that. I will see you and that officer that arrested my boys in court first thing in the morning."

CHAPTER 13

T he next morning, Quincy, Seeley, Jax, Q, and one of Quincy's lawyers arrived at court. By Quincy being a judge, he was able to get the case against Jax and Q moved up to the first one that morning.

Right before the judge came out, Jax went over to the officer that arrested him and Q.

"Officer Stanley, all of this can be stopped, all you have to do is say the word."

Officer Stanley just stared at Jax.

"All RISE!" the bailiff called as the judge came into the courtroom. After the judge sat, everyone sat down as well.

"The state of Kansas City vs Jackson Black and Quincy Black Jr. for car theft. I was looking over this case when I was in my chambers. So let me get this straight, this Officer Stanley arrested these two young black men for stealing a car that apparently is not on the market. Can someone please help me understand this? How can you arrest a person for stealing a car that is not at the dealerships yet? Nor on the market, for that matter? I am trying to wrap my mind around that. How did this nonsense reach the courts?"

"Well, Your Honor—"

"So you mean to tell me that the DA did not find this story suspicious? You know what? I am not even wasting any more of the taxpayers' time or money. I am dismissing this case because what I see is a white cop racially profiling and harassing.

"Mr. Black and Mr. Black, on behalf of the state of Missouri and the police department, I apologize for this misunderstanding. You guys will be getting an apology from the police department.

"As for you, Officer Stanley, you will be suspended without pay, and fined ten thousand dollars. You are lucky that you were not stripped of your badge.

"This court is adjourned."

"See, dude? You should have listened to my brother," Q said as he walked by Officer Stanley. The officer became very furious and started charging at Q, but Jax tripped Officer Stanley, took him by the collar, and slammed him on the table.

"LOOK, DUDE, I GAVE YOU A CHANCE TO GET OUT OF THIS! BUT YOU LET YOUR PRIDE GET IN THE WAY. NOW YOU ARE PISSED BECAUSE A SIXTEEN-YEAR-OLD BOY TOLD YOU WHAT WAS GOING TO HAPPEN.

"NOW, I DON'T CARE IF YOU ARE MAD OR JUST PISSED OFF AT THE WORLD. BUT IF YOU EVER COME AT MY BROTHER LIKE THAT AGAIN, NOT EVEN GOD HIMSELF WILL BE ABLE TO SAVE YOU!"

"JAX! JAX! Calm down! Let Officer Stanley go!"

Quincy Sr. and Seeley had to pull Jax off of Officer Stanley. No charges were filed.

***

After court, Quincy Seeley and the boys went to Quincy's office.

"Jax, Q, I have something to talk to you two about. Seeley and I have been talking about bringing you two on board with our other business."

"What other business do you have, Daddy?"

"Jax, you know what kind of business it is. Don't act so modest and naïve," Quincy said. "I know that you two are kind of young, but this will be good for both of you. It will teach you some discipline, structure. You two are going to have to grow up a little bit. That means Q, you need to start thinking before you speak and act.

"Jax, you are very smart, Son, but when somebody starts messing with your brother, you lose your head and you go crazy. You lost it back there in the courtroom. If you don't learn to control your temper, that could be your downfall. Jax, Q, the wrong move or the wrong mistake could kill you in this business.

"Now, we have a meeting tonight, and I want you both to come and observe. We are going to start training you both. Showing you the ropes and letting you see how things go. So why don't you two head home? I will see you two tonight."

While Q and Jax headed home, Quincy and Seeley stayed back to talk about the meeting and the boys.

"So, Quincy, do think that they will be okay to bring into the fold?"

"Yeah, Seeley, they will be fine. Jax will calm down. Q will too once both of them see how serious this is. They both will straighten up. Is everything set for tonight?"

"Yes sir, just like clockwork Larry called and said that he was not able to meet tonight."

"Well, Seeley, let's find out tonight why Mr. Larry has been missing all of our important meetings."

Quincy headed home and cleared his schedule for the day. He didn't have any cases to oversee, so he wanted to get some rest before the meeting that night. As he was sitting down, Quinn walked into the room.

"Hey, sweetie," Quinn said.

"Hey, babe," Quincy replied.

"How did the boys' court hearing go?"

"Well, Quinn, it went the way that it was supposed to go. The charges were dropped against the boys and the officer was suspended."

"Quincy, I told you not to get that car for Jax! I knew that the police were going to harass him and Q."

"Quinn, relax, it was a good experience for both of them."

"Well, I am just glad that it worked out, then! What time did you come home last night?"

"Quinn, please don't start! I got home around four this morning. I was overseeing a shipping that was coming in."

"Quincy, just be honest with me. I don't see why you keep doing this! I understood when James threatened our lives. I didn't like what was going on, yet I understood what needed to be done. But now it's like all you care about is money and power. You're not the same man that wanted to help this city, that wanted to make a difference!"

"I tried to help this city, I tried to help my community. After a while, I got tired of getting spit on. People, my people, don't want any help. So I started thinking about me and my family. Yes, Quinn, I was thinking just about the money, power as well, because I was in a position to do and be whatever I want to. Becoming the first black man in history to run an all-white Mafia, one of the largest Mafia families in the world—that was something that I just could not pass up!"

"So I suppose selling drugs, running guns, and all of the killing —was it worth the sacrifice? By becoming the Don of Kansas City, you are contributing to killing and selling drugs to your own people."

"Quinn, you can't help people that don't want to be helped!"

"Well, just please be careful. And one more thing: I DON'T WANT THE BOYS MIXED UP IN THIS LIFE! I MEAN IT, QUINCY!"

CHAPTER 14

I t was around 7 o'clock that same night. Quincy was headed to the meeting. He met Seeley in front of the building they were having the meeting at.

"Seeley, is everything in place?"

"Yes sir, everything is in place."

Jax and Q had just arrived as Seeley and Quincy were going into the building.

"Gentlemen, thank you all for coming tonight. Before we get to our regular business, there is an important matter that we need to deal with."

Seeley brought in Larry in his pajamas.

"So, as all of you know, Mr. Larry has missed the last four of our meetings. The reason why he has missed the last four of our meetings is because he has been planning on replacing me."

"Quincy, you dumbass nigger, James should have killed you a long time ago. I'm tired of your arrogant, selfish, righteous ass."

"But Larry, haven't I made you a lot of money? Hell, you even became a billionaire. Everybody in this room did, so why would you want to get rid of me?"

"I AM TIRED OF TAKING ORDERS FROM A NIGGER! QUINCY, IT'S TIME FOR YOU TO GO! WE ALL HAVE DECIDED—"

"Larry, what do mean, *we* have all decided? Hold that thought for one minute! Does anybody else in here want to get rid of me?" Everybody looked around and didn't say a word. "Well, Larry, I think you are on your own with this one."

"QUINCY, IF YOU LAY A FINGER ON ME, YOU AND YOUR FAMILY ARE DEAD! REALLY!"

"Okay! Seeley, do you mind holding Larry's hand for me?"

"Sure, Quincy!"

As Seeley was holding Larry's hand, Quincy started cutting Larry's fingers off. Larry was yelling and screaming.

"YOU BLACK SON OF A BITCH!"

"Here you go, here's your finger on your shoulder! You said if I laid a finger on you, you would have killed me and my family. So I just laid *your* finger on your shoulder."

"QUINCY, YOU F— WAIT UNTIL I GET MY HANDS ON YOU!"

"Hold up!"

Quincy cut the rest of Larry's hand off.

"I AM GOING TO CUT YOUR BLACK, UGLY HEAD OFF."

"Well, Larry, before you say anything thing else, here's a present for you."

Larry opened up the box and found his son's head inside. "OH MY GOD, NOT MY BOY! OH GOD, NO!"

"Now, I have pictures and locations of the schools both of your daughters go to. I even know where your wife is right now. Speaking of your wife." Quincy pulled out a tape of her taking a bath. Quincy even had a lock of her hair for Larry to see. "Damn, Larry, how did an old geezer like you end up with a fine ass woman like that? Lord have mercy."

As Larry was crying and grieving over his son, Quincy said, "Now Larry, let me tell you what's going to happen. You will leave Kansas City tonight. Tell your wife... I don't care what you tell her. You have been trying to figure out how to kill me for years. I have put up with you for years as well, hoping you would finally see things my way. I guess I was naïve! So now you have to go, and if you are not gone by morning, both of your daughters and that beautiful young wife of yours will be mailed to you in pieces.

"Seeley, can you please help Larry to his car, so we can get on with our meeting?"

Seeley helped Larry into his car. Once Larry got inside, someone popped up from the back seat and cut Larry's throat. Seeley and the man then drove the car down to the Bottoms by the river and set the car on fire, burning any and all evidence that Larry had ever existed.

***

After the meeting, Jax and Q were just speechless.

"So Jax, Q, what did you guys think of everything?"

"Well, Daddy, that was a really intense meeting. Was that all necessary? You pretty much tortured that man!"

"Well, Jax, if I hadn't tortured that man, he would have been torturing you, Q, and your mother. Larry was also some unfinished business that needed to be taken care of.

"Okay, boys, besides the Larry incident, what did you guys think of the business?

"It really does sound interesting!" Jax said.

"Well, we want you to start coming up here to the office every day after school, so we can show you how the rest of the business runs."

Jax and Q started going by Quincy's law firm. Quincy and Seeley taught and showed the boys how the business ran. They wanted to make sure that Jax and Q knew how serious this business was.

Jax and Q caught on to the business really quickly. They even figured out where they could earn more money and benefit the organization.

Q and Jax came up with the with the idea of putting up a youth center near every school in all the city. They would start with Kansas City. It would be a youth center for kids to come do activities, sports, and somewhere for the kids to go after school. Yet it would also be an underground drug lab. This would be kept separate from the center. This would be a way to set up shop, yet have it be hidden in plain sight.

If this plan worked like Jax and Q predicted, the Organization would triple their profit. Within the next nine to twelve months they would start the project, getting the first center up. Jax and Q were setting up runs and also getting the center staffed with people they could trust.

Once the center opened, it was an immediate success. It was so successful that Quincy and Seeley started making plans to open more centers across the nation.

Quincy Jr. and Jax were making at least one hundred thousand dollars a week, yet the boys didn't really care about the money they were making. Q was just happy to be working with his father.

Jax also was happy to be working with his father, yet he had thoughts and questions about what his dad was doing. He wondered why his father, a judge, would be doing this. Regardless of the reasoning behind it, Jax was very good at negotiating and selling drugs. Jax knew he was good at it, yet it scared him.

Quincy and Seeley were very impressed with the boys. They were able to run this part of the business, all while going to school.

Quincy's dream was finally coming true. He'd had a dream of him and his two boys running Kansas City. He was showing them everything about the Organization, all of the ins and outs.

"They are really doing a good job, Seeley!"

"Yes, Quincy, they are. I'm very surprised about how quickly they both caught on. Are you thinking about giving them complete control over this part of the business?"

"Actually, I am. Let's keep our eye on Jax and Quincy from a distance."

CHAPTER 15

I t had been a year since Jax and Q built their first center. The boys were a little bit older now. They had a center built in just about every city. Jax and Q were overseeing every delivery and pickup. They put together all of the routes and runs.

Jax came up with a system where people knew only what their jobs were. This way, if someone were to get caught, they would only know what their job was and nobody else's. Jax and Q would be the only two who knew what was going on. Not even Seeley and Quincy knew how the boys' operation was going. Jax figured the less people who knew what was going on, the better.

Q and Jax were bringing in so much money, the Organization was coming close to topping a trillion dollars. Jax and Q's idea was paying off. Things seemed to be going very well. The whole Organization seemed very pleased with Quincy bringing in his two sons. The Organization was becoming the world's number one Mafia. Yet it would not always be like that.

***

"Hey, Q, what time is that meeting, is it at six or eight?"

"I think it's at eight, Jax."

"OK, well let's hurry up and get this done. We need to sit down and go over some more runs. I want to make sure that things are all set before we go on spring break."

"Relax, Jax! What could go wrong? Our security is top-notch and we are extremely careful. We haven't had a raid since we started doing this. We keep certain information between you and me. So what could go wrong?"

"Actually, Q, a lot could wrong. Just please be careful. There are still a couple of weeks before spring break, and before Iesha and I leave for Paris. How many meetings do we have before spring break?"

"We have four: three this week and the fourth one is a couple of days before spring break. That's the one that Uncle Seeley set up with me."

"OK, Q. I will try to go with you to all of the meetings."

Q and Jax had become major distributors in the Midwest. They were gaining popularity and being noticed from all over the globe.

***

"Hey Q, what day and time is the next meeting?"

"Actually, it's today in about one hour."

"Do you want me to go with you?"

"Go get ready to go to Paris, bro. I got this, I can handle it."

"OK, Q. If you need me, just call. I'm not leaving for a couple days."

"Jax, stop worrying!"

"Well, bro, I will see you when I get back."

"OK, Jax, have fun, but not too much fun.

Q went to the meeting; he took five men with him for security. The man that Q was meeting with was called Lodi. He was from Jamaica and was very dangerous.

"So, you're Q Black, huh?"

"Yes sir! You must be Lodi. It's nice to meet you."

"So, Mr. Black, where is that product that you have for me?"

"Well, Lodi, I have what you asked for. For someone that's buying product from us for the first time, you are really buying a lot! Here are your one hundred thousand keys. That will be forty million dollars," Q said.

Just as Q said that, Lodi started laughing. "Look here, man, I'm not paying that much for this blow. All I am going to give you for this is one million dollars."

"Lodi, I don't know what you heard, but huh we don't play around when it comes to selling product. So if you want to buy this product, then the price is going to be forty million."

"Look here, little boy, I am only paying one million for this. Now you can take the money or we can just take the blow from you."

"WHAT DID YOU JUST SAY? DID YOU SAY YOU WERE GOING TO TAKE THIS FROM ME?"

"YES, STUCK-UP LITTLE PUSSY!"

Lodi and his men pulled guns on Q and his men. Q punched Lodi and took his gun from him. He shot two of Lodi's men. Then he put the gun to Lodi's head.

"OK, now you just pissed me off! Obviously you have no idea who I am or who my father is. So let me tell you how this meeting is going to go. You are going to take the rest of your men, and get the hell out of my city tonight, or you won't live to see another sunset in Jamaica or anywhere else."

Lodi and the rest of the men left without saying a word. Q cleaned up and took the product back to the safe house where they normally keep it.

Afterwards, Q went to a couple of parties, but besides that Q just stayed home with a couple of friends. They played video games and hung out with Quinn and Quincy when Quincy was at home.

Q was taking a break from the business, at least until Jax got back. He was really enjoying not going to school or rushing trying to oversee how the product was being packed and taken out. Even though he was a successful drug dealer, he was still a teenager.

Q and Quinn were planning on having a movie night, just the two of them. Quinn was making dinner. She sent Q out to get something from the store.

Q pulled into the parking lot and parked. When he came out of the store, two guys threw a bag over Q's head and threw him in a van. They took him to an abandoned warehouse down in the Bottoms and pulled him out of the van.

"WHAT THE HELL ARE YOU GUYS DOING? GET THIS GOD-DAMN BAG OFF ME!" Q kept yelling and screaming. When they took him into the warehouse and took the bag off his head, he saw Lodi.

"SO WHAT? YOU TOO MUCH OF A BITCH TO COME WHIP A SIXTEEN-YEAR-OLD'S ASS? Huh, Lodi?"

"Boy, you talk more shit for somebody that's about to get their ass kicked. Hell, I might even kill you!"

"Well, bring it on, pussy, I'm not backing down."

Q got loose and grabbed one of Lodi's men's gun. He managed to shoot and kill at least three of Lodi's men before Lodi shot Q three times. Lodi beat and tortured Q, and after they were done, they left him there in the abandoned warehouse.

Seeley got word that one of their men was beaten almost to death. He went by to see who it was. When he went into the warehouse, he saw Q lying there, barely breathing. He immediately called Quincy and told him what had happened. Quincy couldn't believe what Seeley was telling him.

When Quincy saw Q, tears started rolling down his eyes.

"SOMEBODY GET A DAMN AMBULANCE, DON'T JUST STAND THERE! GET SOME GODDAMN HELP!

Seeley had to pull Quincy to the side to calm him down.

"Quincy, I got a chopper coming to airlift him to the hospital. You have to calm down, so pull yourself together so you can call and tell Quinn."

Quincy pulled himself together and rode with Seeley to the hospital. They rushed Q into the emergency room. Quincy couldn't take his eyes off his baby boy.

"Quincy, you need to call Quinn, tell her what happened."

"Seeley, I don't know how to tell her this!"

Quincy finally called Quinn, who said, "Hey, sweetie, have you seen Q? I sent him to the store to pick up some things for me to finish cooking."

"Quinn, Q is in the hospital. He was shot, beaten, and left for dead."

"WHAT! QUINCY, WHAT THE HELL HAPPENED TO MY BABY?"

"QUINN, YOU NEED TO GET TO THE HOSPITAL *NOW*!"

Quinn got to the hospital as fast as she could. She pulled into the front of the hospital and ran inside. She didn't even park the car. One of Seeley's men had to park the car for her.

Quinn ran towards Q and immediately started crying and screaming. Quincy had to take Quinn out of the room to calm her down.

While Quinn and Quincy were in the waiting room, Quinn asked Quincy a question.

"Quincy, what happened to my child? Why would anyone want to hurt Q? Please don't tell me that you pulled Q and Jax into that lifestyle. QUINCY, PLEASE DON'T TELL ME THAT YOU GOT BOTH OF MY BOYS SELLING DRUGS! IS MY BABY LYING IN THIS HOSPITAL BED BECAUSE OF A DEAL GONE BAD?"

"I'm not sure, but I think so, Quinn."

Quinn slapped Quincy.

"You bastard! MY BABY IS LYING UP HERE IN THE HOSPITAL BECAUSE OF SOME SHIT YOU GOT HIM INTO!"

"Quinn, I will find the people who did this to Q. I promise you I will."

Quinn went back in the room to be with Q.

Quincy looked over at Seeley.

"Seeley, can you please call Jax, find out where he is, and make sure that he's OK."

Seeley called Jax.

"Hello!"

"Hey, Uncle Seeley!"

"Jax, there is something I have to tell you. You brother has been shot."

CHAPTER 16

"**U**NLCE SEELEY, WHAT DO YOU MEAN Q WAS SHOT! WHAT HAPPENED TO MY BROTHER?"

"Jax, where are you at?"

"I just got off the plane. I am at the airport with Iesha."

"OK, Jax, stay there. I'm on my way to get both of you."

Seeley went to the airport and picked up Jax and Iesha. They all headed back to the hospital.

Iesha and Jax walked into Q's hospital room.

"Oh my God," Iesha said as she started crying. Jax just looked at his brother as tears started to run down from his eyes.

Quincy came in and saw Jax and Iesha in the room with Quinn. He stepped back out in the hallway. "Seeley, please tell me that you found them."

"I'm sorry, Quincy, I haven't found them yet."

"HOW HARD CAN IT BE TO FIND OUT WHO DID THIS TO MY SON?"

"Quincy, we are looking all over the city!"

"I DON'T CARE WHO YOU KILL, PAY OFF, WHOSE HEAD YOU HAVE TO CUT OFF! FIND OUT WHO DID THIS TO MY SON."

"OK, Quincy, we will keep looking."

Quincy went back into the room with everybody else and whispered into Jax's ear, "Son, we really need to talk."

Jax just looked at his father and walked out of the room into the hallway. He made a phone call to one of his father's tech guys, whose name was Henry. He had been working with Jax and Q.

"Henry."

"Hey, Jax, I heard what happened. I figured you would be calling me."

"Did my father or my uncle call you yet?"

"No, not yet, Jax, but I'm quite sure they will."

"OK. Henry, do you have the GPS coordinates of Q's last meeting, along with the feeds?"

"I have all of that. I even have the feeds and recordings of the day when he was kidnapped."

"Good, Henry, that's very good."

Jax received the information from Henry. It took him no more than an hour to find Lodi.

Jax went to the house where Lodi and the rest of his men were staying. He had enough weapons and firepower to level at least two city blocks.

Jax threw some smoke gas around the house. Lodi and his men were stunned, trying to figure out what was going on.

Jax began taking out Lodi's men. There were four in the front of the house. Jax came up from behind one of them, broke his leg, then cut off the guy's head. He threw acid on the next guy's face and then put a gun in the guy's month and blew the guy's brains out. The next two, Jax tore apart—literally.

When Jax got inside, he had a sword with him. He cut up all of the rest of Lodi's men. It had to have been at least six or seven men in the house. There were arms, legs, and heads flying everywhere, and so much blood.

When he got to Lodi, Jax was covered in blood.

"You're Lodi, right?" Jax asked.

"Come on, man, it's just business, you taking this too personal. I didn't kill the boy, it was only a message." Lodi kept pleading for his life.

First Jax just cut off Lodi's hand. Then he cut off Lodi's other arm. Then he cut Lodi up piece by piece. He wanted to make sure that Lodi felt everything.

After Jax got done cutting up Lodi, he just sat there waiting for the police. He was getting ready to make an anonymous phone call to the police, to tell them what happened.

Before he could do that, Seeley pulled up to the house and saw all of the dead bodies in front of the house. He went inside with his gun out, thinking that someone was still there. He slowly walked in and saw Jax sitting on the table.

"OH MY GOD! Jax, are you OK?"

Jax would not say a word.

"Jax! Jax! Did you call anybody?"

He just shook his head no.

Seeley immediately called Quincy and told him exactly what happened.

"Are you serious, Seeley?" Quincy asked.

When Quincy got off the phone, he was in such shock.

"Quincy, what's wrong? Why do you look like that?"

"Quinn... I... I have to go! I will tell you when I get back."

"Quincy! Quincy!" Quinn called his name while he just kept walking. *What the hell is going on?* Quinn asked herself.

"Iesha, did Jax tell you where he was going?"

"No ma'am, I didn't even know he was gone. I just tried to call him and I didn't get any answer."

"Yeah, Iesha, I just tried to call him too."

While Quinn and Iesha were trying to find Jax, Quincy pulled up in front of the house where Jax was. He got out of his car and couldn't believe what he saw. Body parts were everywhere; it looked like a scene from a horror movie.

"Quincy, over here!"

"Seeley, are you sure Jax did all of this?"

"Yes, Quincy, I am quite sure. When you see Jax, you will see why."

Quincy went to the other room and saw Jax covered in so much blood.

"Jax, are you OK, Son?"

Jax was in so much shock that he barely said anything.

"Seeley, I can't believe that Jax would do something like this. How did Jax find Lodi and his men so quickly?"

"I couldn't begin to tell you how. All I know is while we were looking for Lodi, I got a call telling me to check this house out. When I did, that's when I found Jax sitting there, shocked."

"Seeley, we have to contain this. Get a cleaning crew in here stat. Try to keep this quiet as long as you can."

"Quincy, I have killed my share of people and I have seen people killed before. What Jax did, I've never seen anything like it. This was a massacre!"

Quincy and Seeley went over to talk to Jax.

"Jax, Son, let go of the sword. Let's go and get you cleaned up, OK?"

Quincy and Seeley led Jax to the car with a towel wrapped around him.

"Quinn is going to kill me," Quincy told Seeley. He called her to tell her what had happened.

"Quinn, sweetie, I got some more bad news for you."

"QUINCY, WHAT IN THE HELL DO YOU MEAN, YOU HAVE SOME BAD NEWS?"

"It's Jax. Jax found the men that beat and almost killed Q. He tortured and killed all of them by himself. When Seeley found him, he was covered in blood and in shock. Quinn, I have never seen anything like this. It was a massacre! There were body parts all over the place."

"QUINCY, I TOLD YOUR ASS THAT I DIDN'T WANT MY BOYS WRAPPED UP IN THIS MESS. NOW Q IS IN THE HOSPITAL AND YOU DONE TURNED JAX INTO A KILLER. MY POOR BABY IS PROBABLY TRAUMATIZED. QUINCY, JUST TELL ME WHERE MY SON IS. YOU'VE DONE ENOUGH ALREADY!"

"Quinn!"

"DON'T YOU 'QUINN' ME, QUINCY! JUST TELL ME WHERE JAX IS GOING!"

"He's headed to the house! I sent a doctor to the house to have him checked out. Quinn…Quinn…! Damn!"

"Quincy, what's wrong?"

"Well, Quinn is not happy with me! She just hung up the phone."

"Quinn hung up on you? Damn, dude, she is pissed!"

Quincy and Seeley took Jax to the house and Quinn and Iesha met them there.

"OH MY GOD! JAX!" Quinn yelled after she saw him.

Iesha was just speechless.

"Iesha, take Jax to his room so we can get those bloody clothes off him. Let's also wash him up as well," Quinn ordered.

Iesha led Jax to his room and helped him get his clothes off. She also wiped the blood off Jax's face and the rest of his body.

"Jax, it's me, Iesha. Are you OK? Jax, it's me, baby. Please say something."

Jax just looked at Iesha and started crying.

"Jax, it's OK, baby, it's going to be OK."

While Iesha was trying to calm down Jax, Quincy and Quinn were having a very heated conversation.

"Quincy..."

"JUST DON'T START, I DON'T WANT TO HEAR IT!"

"WELL, QUINCY, I DONT'T GIVE A DAMN IF YOU WANT TO HEAR ME OR NOT! WHAT WERE YOU THINKING, BRINGING THEM INTO ALL THAT MESS?"

"QUINN, I KNOW WHAT I AM DOING!"

"IF YOU KNEW WHAT YOU WERE DOING, THEN Q WOULD NOT BE IN THE HOSPITAL! JAX WOULD NOT HAVE KILLED ANY-BODY! YOU NEED TO FIX THIS!"

"WHAT DO YOU MEAN, I HAVE TO FIX THIS?"

"REALLY, QUINCY? *YOU* ARE THE REASON WHY MY BOYS ARE IN THIS PREDICAMENT! NOW YOUR BLACK ASS NEEDS TO FIX IT!"

CHAPTER 17

While Quinn and Quincy were finishing up their heated conversation, Iesha had just gotten Jax to go to bed.

Iesha knocked on Quinn and Quincy's door.

"Mrs. Black, it's Iesha. I just put Jax to sleep!"

Quinn opened the door and came out of the room.

"Hey, Iesha, could you please stay the night? I know that's kind of weird, your boyfriend's mother asking you, his girlfriend, to stay over. Right now he needs somebody that he loves, somebody besides me and his father. I will call your mother and talk to her."

"Sure, Mrs. Black, I can stay tonight."

Iesha went to take a shower, but while she was in the shower, Jax woke up, got dressed, and left.

"Jax! Jax!" Iesha called Jax's name, trying to find him when she got out of the shower. Quinn heard Iesha calling Jax's name. She went upstairs to find out what was going on.

"Iesha, what's wrong, why are you calling Jax's name?"

"Mrs. Black, I don't know where Jax is at!"

"What are you talking about? Jax is sleep. I checked on him about twenty minutes ago while you were in the shower."

"When I came out of the bathroom, he was gone."

"Where could he have gone this time of night?"

"I don't know, Mrs. Black. I've been calling him, but he's not picking up his phone."

"GODDAMN IT! I need to call Quincy!"

While Quinn and Iesha were looking for Jax, Jax was driving around trying to clear his head. He was trying to forget what he did. Every time he closed his eyes, that's all he would see.

Jax kept driving around, and he saw a light on at a church, so he stopped to see if it was open. It was around three thirty in the morning. Jax figured that the church would be closed, yet he was hoping it was not.

"Son, it's kind of late, but how can I help you?"

"Father, right?" Jax asked.

"Yes, son, that's right. Is there something bothering you, son?"

"Yes, Father, there is. I don't know how this works. I belong to a baptized church," Jax said.

"Son, I'm not just your pastor, I'm a Servant of God. I'm a good listener as well."

"OK, Father, here goes. When I came back from my spring vacation trip, I found out that my brother was attacked, beaten, and shot three times and left for dead. I lost it. I found the people that were responsible for it. I SHOWED NO MERCY, I KILLED ALL OF THEM! I SLAUGHTERED EVERY LAST ONE OF THEM. THERE WAS NOTHING BUT BODY PARTS! WHEN I GOT TO THE LEADER, I JUST STARTED TO CUT HIM. AFTER I STARTED, I JUST COULDN'T STOP. I JUST KEPT CUTTING AND CHOPPING. I CUT HIM INTO PIECES. WHEN MY FATHER AND UNCLE FOUND ME, I WAS COVERED IN BLOOD. SINCE THAT HAPPENED, I CAN'T EAT OR SLEEP.

"I feel like I'll become a monster if I continue to stay here in Kansas City working with my father. I'm scared of what I might become. I'm seventeen years old, and I graduate in two months. My father wants me to stay here and go to KU to study law. I

CAN'T STAY HERE, I HAVE TO LEAVE."

"Well, my son, I can only imagine what you must be going through! What you did was very wrong. But you already know that. You have to ask God to forgive you. Most importantly, you have to try to find a way to forgive yourself. Until you do that, you will never find peace. It's going to be okay, just let me say a prayer.

"Heavenly Father, we come to you, first of all saying thanks. Thank you for allowing another day, Father God. I ask that you look on this man! Forgive him for what he has done. Please, Heavenly Father. Most importantly, Father, allow him to forgive himself. Please, Father, in the name of Jesus we pray. Amen.

"Son, remember you have to start forgiving yourself. If you can't do that, this guilt is going to tear you apart."

Jax went back to the house. Quinn, Iesha, and Quincy were calling all over, trying to find Jax to make sure that he was OK. As Jax walked in the door, Quinn yelled, "Jax, WHERE IN THE HELL HAVE YOU BEEN?"

"Sorry, Mama, I had to get out and clear my head."

"Jax, honey, the next time you want to go and clear your head, just let somebody know where you are going."

"OK, Mama, I will next time."

"Are you OK?"

"I just need to get some sleep. I will be fine, I just need some rest."

Iesha stayed in his room to make sure that he was alright, but Jax still could not get any sleep.

When she woke up, Iesha asked, "Jax, sweetie, how are you feeling?"

"I am OK, Iesha. Did you sleep OK?"

"Yes I did, I slept like a baby. Did you get any sleep, Jax?"

"No, Iesha, I didn't!"

"Are you OK?"

"Yes, I will be fine, I just need some time, that's all. I am about to get dressed and head up to the hospital to see Q."

"OK, let me take a shower and change, and I will go up there with you."

While Jax and Iesha were getting ready to go see Q, Quincy was at his office with Seeley.

"Seeley, were you able to find out why Q was kidnapped and attacked?"

"Well, Quincy, it appears like it was a deal gone wrong from all the info that I'm gathering. I also think that Q pissed off Lodi as well. I told you, Quincy, I told you Q was still a hothead."

"Yeah, I know, Seeley, but they kidnapped him, shot him, and then beat him half to death. There's got to be more to the story."

"I will keep digging to see what I can find out. You might want to talk to Jax; he might be the only one that can give us some answers."

"Let's wait until Q wakes up so we can talk to him," Quinn said.

Meanwhile, Jax and Iesha had headed up to the hospital to see Q. He was conscious and was trying to talk, yet Q was still too weak.

"Iesha, if only I had been there or gone to that meeting with him...."

"Then both of you would be in the hospital."

"I do know one thing, Iesha: I will find out who was behind this. Mark my words!"

CHAPTER 18

It had been almost three weeks since Q was jumped and Jax slaughtered Lodi and all of his men. Q was awake and getting stronger. He went to physical therapy every day, trying to learn how to walk. It was a slow process, but Q was getting better by the day.

Jax was still having trouble sleeping and eating, yet he was able to talk about what happened without breaking down. But Jax was clear about one thing: he knew that if he stayed in Kansas City, that he would become a monster, something or someone that he would not recognize. He was scared that he would do something a lot worse than what he did that night.

"Hey, Jax, can we talk for a minute?"

"Sure, Mama!"

"Sweetie, I really haven't had a chance to sit down with you. How are you doing?"

"I'm doing OK, considering everything that happened."

"Jax, are you sure you are OK?"

"Mama, I'm OK, but there is something that I have to tell you. I've been thinking of a way to tell you for the past two weeks."

"What is it, Jackson?"

"Mama, ever since that night happened, it kind of scared me. I know that you are mad at Daddy for pulling Q and me into his underground world. Don't be mad at him, we could have said no. It was just so fun. It wasn't about the money or power. For me it was more like creating something with my brother. Something that we started.

"When Q got jumped, and I saw him in that hospital bed, I snapped. After I killed all of those men, I realized that I was turning into a monster. I didn't like it. I *don't* like it, Mama. I can't stay in Kansas City anymore. If I do stay, I *will* turn into a monster, something a lot worse than the other night. I already received my acceptance letter from Harvard. I'm leaving in two weeks after graduation."

"Have you told your father and brother yet?"

"No, not yet. I was going to tell Q sometime this week. As far as telling Daddy, I don't know when or how I'm going to tell him."

"Jax, this is your life. If you want to go to Harvard instead of KU, then go. But you have to tell your father how you feel. You have to talk to him. I already know that there's no stopping Q from continuing to work with your father. Even after he is well and back on his feet, he's going to go back and start selling drugs again. He's more like your father than anything in that regard. Although Q listens to you, Jax. Have you tried—"

"Mama, there's no use. Q does like the power; he likes the fact that he's overseeing something, especially at a young age. So instead of me stopping him, I was going to help him with the books. While I'm doing that, maybe I can try and talk him out of it."

"Well, we'll see."

"Mama, I'm about to go and visit Q at the hospital, do you want to come?"

"No, Jax, you go ahead, I have some work to catch up on."

Jax went to the hospital to check and see how Q was doing. When he got there, Q was just getting back from his physical therapy.

"Jax, how long have you been waiting on me?"

"Not long, Q. How are you feeling?"

"Man, this physical therapy stuff sucks!"

"Well, Q, the more you keep doing it, the stronger you will get. Then you will be able to walk out of here! So hush up and get better.

"Now, listen, Q, I need to know who set up the meeting with you and Lodi."

"Uncle Seeley did, Jax. I thought you knew that. Uncle Seeley called me and told me that he had a friend that would like to buy some product from us. He sent me the info and set up the meeting. Why are you asking?"

"Q, somebody set you up. I looked at the video feed. Lodi already knew that you were not going to sell him that much weight for that small of a price. He went to that meeting with a mind of hurting or trying to kill you."

"How do you know all of that?"

"Think about it, Q, just think of how he was acting, how he wasn't surprised when you told him no."

"Jax, quit stressing over them ASSHOLES you killed. It's over!"

"Somebody set you up, and I'm going to find out who did it. By the way, there is something that I have to tell you."

"What's that, Jax?"

"I'm leaving KC."

"Why?"

"Because that night I killed Lodi, I didn't just kill Lodi—I slaughtered his whole crew. Q, I just flipped out. I remember everything that I did, all of those body parts flying everywhere. I just can't stay here, bro. If I stay here, I'm afraid of what I might become. I don't want to turn into a monster or a killer. I hope you can understand, Q."

"Jax, I get it, and I do understand. I will always love you, bro. I can only imagine what you are going through. So if that's what you have to do to get peace of mind, then do it."

"Thanks for understanding. Before I go, I will help you get back on your feet. All of the centers are still bringing in some serious cash. But we need to come up with a better system so something like this will not happen again."

"OK, Jax, I'm down for that."

"OK, enough of that. Has Iesha been up here?"

"Not yet. She said she was going to be here after school today."

"Well, school isn't out yet, so I will go pick her up and we will be back up here later on."

"OK, bro, I will see you in a little bit. Oh yeah, Jax, you might want to talk to Daddy about you leaving. You know he's not going to be happy about that!"

"Yeah, I know, Q. I will talk to him soon."

***

Jax went to pick up Iesha from school.

"Hey, sweetie!"

"Hey, baby!"

"How was your day at school?"

"Well, it was cool, except everybody was asking about you and Q. I think everybody knows what happened to Q. They don't know what you did, but they know about Q being in the hospital."

"Well, as long as they just know what happened to Q, then that's all they need to know."

"Oh yeah, can you stop by your house? I promised Q that I would bring his PlayStation up to him."

"Iesha, Q can wait. I need to talk to you about something."

"What is it?"

"Iesha, I'm not going to KU after we graduate. I'm going to Harvard."

"Why are you going to Harvard? I thought you were going to KU with me."

"You know why I'm going to Harvard. I have to get away from here. Why don't you come with me?"

"I can't come with you to Harvard."

"If you need help…"

"Jax, I can't keep asking your family for help."

"Stop it! You know my dad doesn't mind helping you. Please, Iesha, just think about it."

"I will go."

"Are you for real?"

"Yes, Jax, I will go to Harvard with you."

Jax made his rounds, telling everybody that he cared about that he was leaving Kansas City. Even though Jax was leaving for Harvard, he was still trying to figure out who set up Q. Even though he would not be selling drugs with his brother, he wanted to know what was going on, and he was going to get to the truth one way or the other.

CHAPTER 19

A month had passed. Q's physical therapy was going very well. He still needed some work, but besides all that he was doing really good. Q wanted to be able to go to Jax's graduation and his going-away party.

Jax and Iesha visited Q every day after school to help him with his schoolwork and other business.

Quinn was getting the party ready for Jax and Iesha. When Jax came home, his father was there, which was kind of strange, because Quincy never came home around that time. This was Jax's chance to talk to Quincy.

Jax went to Quincy's study.

"Hey, Daddy, do you have a minute? I want to talk to you."

"Sure, Jax, what's up?"

"Daddy, I want to let you know that I won't be going to KU. I am going to Harvard. I will be leaving a week after graduation to pick my classes for summer."

"Jax, what happened to you going to KU?"

"Daddy, I can't stay here in Kansas City. Ever since that night, I can't sleep, I barely can eat. I have a hard time focusing. I can't do this type of business anymore. I can't continue to sell drugs."

"But it will be different. We will increase security, we will fix it so that nothing like this will ever happen again, I promise."

"Daddy, you can't promise something like that. When you are going to meetings like that, selling and buying product, there's no guarantee what could happen at those meetings. If I killed that many people when Q was hurt, I'm scared of what I might do if, you, Mama, or Iesha ever got hurt like that. I don't want to become that person, that monster."

"Jax, you have to let that go."

"HOW CAN I LET SOMETHING LIKE THAT GO?!"

"JAX, WHO IN THE HELL ARE YOU RISING YOUR VOICE AT?"

"I'm sorry, Daddy, I didn't mean to disrespect you like that. I just can't do it anymore. I just can't."

"Son, wait a minute, what can I do to get you to stay?"

"Step down from being head of the Organization. Daddy, you are the richest judge in America. You are a billionaire—hell, you are worth billions. You could finish your term and retire. You don't need the money."

"Son, I'm afraid I can't do that."

"WHY NOT?"

"Jax, you wouldn't understand."

"Well, Daddy, I can't stay! I'm sorry, Daddy."

Quincy just looked at Jax and walked out of the study. Jax shook his head. He thought he could talk to his dad into stepping away from that type of life. Yet he was wrong.

Jax went to his room to start packing. He would be leaving the day right after graduation. As Jax was packing, Quinn knocked on his door before she entered his room.

"Jax, can I come in?"

"Sure, Mama, I'm just packing, that's all."

"Did you talk to your father?"

"Yes, Mama, I did. I tried to make him understand. But he didn't want to. He was very disappointed that I wasn't going to KU. He asked what he could do to get me to stay. I asked him to step down from being the head of the Organization. He just looked at me and said that he couldn't do that. When I told him that I couldn't stay in Kansas City, he just walked out of the study."

"Jax, sweetie, I'm so sorry about your father. He's been in the Organization for twenty-five years now. He's not going to give up that power, not even for you, Jax."

"It's okay, Mama, I'm looking forward to going to Massachusetts."

"Well, I can't wait to show you around. You will love it up there."

Quinn helped Jax finish packing. After they were done, they both went up to the hospital to see how Q was doing.

"Hey bro, how are you feeling?"

"I'm ready to get the hell out of here!"

"Q, watch your mouth!"

"Sorry, Mama, but I seriously am ready to go!"

"Quincy Junior., the doctor said he will release you within the next few days, depending on your progress, so please be patient."

"Hey, Jax, when are you leaving for Massachusetts?"

"Next week, the day after graduation."

Right after Jax told Q that, the doctor came in and told Q that he could go home during the afternoon. Jax and Quinn got all of his stuff ready and helped Q get dressed so he could leave the hospital.

Q was so happy to be going home. The whole idea was for Q to go home, to get comfortable and used to walking around the home again so they could see how he did before he could go anywhere else.

It took Q a couple of days, but the day before Jax's graduation,

Q was walking and getting around a lot better than expected. On the special day, everybody in the family showed up for Jax's graduation.

After Jax and Iesha had received their diplomas, they left the ceremony and met up with their families. They went back to the house, where Quinn and Quincy threw Jax and Iesha a graduation party. Everybody was there having a good time. Some of Jax and Iesha's friends stopped by after the graduation. Even Quincy was having a good time, despite the tension between him and Jax.

While everybody was having a good time, Iesha asked Jax if she could talk to him for a little bit, so they went up to his room.

"Jax, there is something that I have to tell you." Iesha was trying to hold back tears.

"Iesha, what is it?"

"I can't go with you to Harvard!"

"Why not?"

"I overheard my parents talking a couple days ago. My dad is losing his job. My mother will be picking up extra shifts until he finds another job. My dad has no other experience besides working in a factory. He didn't finish high school. So I told them last night that I was going to stay here, go to KU so I can help out my with my brother and sisters. Also, I'll help out with the bills as much as I can. I will be going to school on Tuesdays and Thursdays, and taking some classes online as well. The reason I'm crying is because I know that you will probably break up with me for doing this to you all of a sudden. I am so sorry, baby."

"Iesha, do you really think that I am that much of an ASSHOLE? I totally understand. I hate that you are not going to Massachusetts with me, but I understand you have to be there with your family. We will make this work. If you need anything, just let me know. If you want to, I can talk to my Dad, see if he could get your dad a job."

"Jax, you my dad would never take a job from your father. He's too proud for that."

"If he changes his mind, just let me know."

"That's why I love you, Jax."

"Iesha, can you go up to Massachusetts with me tomorrow? Please!"

"Yes, Jax, of course I will go."

The next day, Quincy, Quinn, and Iesha took a flight with Jax to Massachusetts. Jax's things had already been sent ahead of him. Jax wanted to get there to pick his classes for the summer and get his dorm room settled before he started school. He wanted somewhere to go when there weren't any classes, in case he didn't want to go back to Kansas City for his break.

After Jax got his classes and dorm room straightened out, Quinn wanted to show Jax around where she grew up. She also wanted to stop by Professor Williams's office and see how he was doing.

"Hey, Professor Williams," Quinn greeted as she and her husband walked into the professor's office.

"Quinn, Quincy, OH MY GOD. I thought you two had thrown me away."

"Never that, Professor Williams, never that!" Quincy said.

"So, what brings you two here to Harvard?"

"Well, Professor, our son will be coming here in a couple of weeks," Quinn said.

"Really! Well, Quinn, where is he at?"

Jax and Iesha were in the hallway talking to some fellow students.

Quinn went out and brought him in to meet Professor Williams.

"Well, I say you look just like Quincy! I hope you are smart like your mother!"

"I heard that, Professor Williams!" Quincy said.

"Your name is Jackson, right, son?"

"Yes, Professor Williams, but I go by Jax!"

"Jax, stop by my office sometime, then I will be able to tell you all about your mother's secrets," the professor said as he laughed. Jax started laughing as well.

"Professor Williams, what secrets are you talking about?" Quinn asked.

Professor Williams just looked at her.

"Oh yeah, those secrets."

"Quinn, what are you and Professor Williams talking about?"

"Nothing, honey!" Quinn said, and kissed Quincy on the lips innocently.

Quinn and Quincy invited Professor Williams to lunch with them before they headed back to Kansas City. As they were all eating and having a good time, Quincy looked at his watch and said that they needed to get going.

"It sure was nice for you two to stop and visit with me. Don't worry about Jax while he's here; I will keep my eye on him."

They said their goodbyes and Quincy, Quinn, Jax, and Iesha headed back to Kansas City.

When they arrived, Quincy wanted to talk to Jax for a little bit.

"Jax, I heard that you are helping your brother with some parts of the business?"

"All I'm doing is helping him get back on his feet. I will give him a little advice about the books when he needs some help."

"Son, you do realize that you're not really walking away from the business. You are still going to be involved in the business by helping your brother."

"Daddy, I'm out, I'm not selling drugs anymore."

"OK, Son, we will see!"

CHAPTER 20

J ax was very busy getting ready to go to Harvard. He had a lot of things he needed to get done before his classes started.

Iesha was headed down to KU the following day, to get settled in her dorm. Jax want to ride down with her and to help her unpack, so Jax rolled down to KU with Iesha and her parents. He wanted to spend a little time with Iesha before he left for Massachusetts.

Iesha's parents told Jax and Iesha to go and have lunch. They were going to finish unpacking Iesha's stuff.

"So, Mr. Black, are you going to miss me?" Iesha asked as they ate.

"Really, Iesha, what kind of question is that? Of course I'm going to miss you."

"You better behave while you are up there in Massachusetts, Jax."

"I should be telling *you* that, Ms. Iesha."

"Are you going to be OK? I know that you are still having nightmares."

"I'll be OK, Iesha, I'm just taking one day at a time. That's part of the reason why I'm leaving and going to Massachusetts. I need a break from my father. If I were to go to KU, I know for a fact that I would just be slipping deeper into the business with father. I'm scared of the man, or rather monster, that I am turning into. I have to get away from this. I have to at least try!"

"Jax, if you are going to help Q with the books, with that part of the business, then you are not really getting out of the business. You are still dealing with it!"

"All I am doing is helping Q get back on his feet. While I'm doing that, I thought maybe I could talk to him. May I could get him to stop. I know it's a long shot. But I have to try."

"I have never seen anyone love their brother as much as you do. That's why I fell in love with you. The love you have for your family and friends is so beautiful."

"Well, Iesha, don't you ever forget that. I love you too." Jax kissed Iesha. "Hey, let's go find your parents. I have to get home so I can finish packing and go over some things with Q."

After Jax and Iesha found Iesha's parents, Jax gave Iesha a big hug and kiss, and Jax and her parents rode back together.

Once Jax was back in his house, he went upstairs to his room to finish packing. After he got done packing, Q walked into his room.

"Hey Jax, I was about to go over all the details and new procedures with Henry. So, the only ones that will be on the inner circle will be you, me, and Henry." Since Jax would be in Massachusetts, they needed someone that they knew they could trust in.

After Q, Jax, and Henry had gotten everything straightened out, Jax was making the last arrangements for the rest of his things to be sent to Massachusetts. Jax still had some worry in the back of his head. He was still trying to figure out who had set up Q. He told Henry to keep his ear open, yet to do it quietly, as he did not want any of this getting back to his father or Seeley.

The time came for Jax to go. Quinn went downstairs and gave Jax a big hug and kiss. She told him to not forget to go by and see his grandparents.

"Q, Mom, I will talk to you in a couple of weeks."

"OK, bro, be careful," Q said as they embraced each other.

Just as Jax was getting ready to walk out the door, Quincy rumbled, "Jackson Black, you're not going to leave here without saying goodbye to your father, are you?" A big smile came across Jax's face.

As Jax turned around, Quincy told Jax, "We are not always going to see eye to eye. We will argue. But I will always be daddy, you will always be my son. You have turned out to be a fine young man. I have to respect that. I will always love you, Son. Don't you ever forget that."

"I love you too, Daddy." Quincy gave Jax a big hug.

It was time for Jax to head to the airport. He boarded the plane.

When he got to Massachusetts, he went to his dorm and gazed out the balcony, looking at the campus. He said to himself, "I can finally find some peace."

***

Several years had passed. By this time, Jax had graduated from Harvard and Harvard Law School at the top of his class. In just under two years, he was able to start his own firm, which grew so big that Jax was thinking about opening up another office.

Jax had just gotten home from a long day at the office. He poured himself a glass of smooth Scotch. He looked out over the balcony of his penthouse and said to himself, "I did it! I'm finally at peace with myself. In my city! My city!"

Just as he said that, the phone rang.

"Hey Jax, this is Q. Daddy's been shot!"

"WHAT DO YOU MEAN, DADDY'S BEEN SHOT?!"

"I don't know what happened! I am on my way to the hospital. Mama is already on her way to the hospital as well."

"Q, call Iesha and have her meet Mama up there. I am heading to the airport right now. I should be there within two hours."

"Are you sure you want me to call Iesha?"

"Just call her! I will be there as soon as I can!"

Jax got to the airport and boarded a plane. While Jax was waiting for the plane to leave, he made a phone call to Henry and asked him to get some information.

Meanwhile, back in Kansas City, Seeley had just gotten home. As he opened his door and turned on the lights, he jumped when he saw Jax sitting on one of his chairs in the dark.

"Jax, Jesus, you scared me!"

"Sorry, Uncle Seeley, I wasn't trying to!"

"When did you get in town?"

"About an hour ago. I thought you would be at the hospital, Uncle Seeley."

"At the hospital for what, Jax?"

"Daddy's been shot!"

"OH MY GOD! LET'S GET TO THE HOSPITAL!"

Seeley turned around and Jax pulled a gun out and held it up to his head. Seely looked up and said, "Jax, what are you doing?"

"Uncle Seeley, we are going to sit right here until you tell me why you set up Q and Daddy. We are not leaving here until you do!"

Made in the USA
Middletown, DE
09 August 2022

70961210R00061